PREHISTORIC

CLOCK

Robert Appleton

This book is a work of fiction. Characters, names, places and incidents either are the product of the author's imagination or are used fictitiously, and any resemblance to any actual persons, living or dead, events, or locales is entirely coincidental.

PREHISTORIC CLOCK

ISBN- 979-8700735353

Printed in the United States of America

Copyright @ Robert Appleton 2021

Published by Mercury Seven Books

A special thank you to my intrepid editor and airship co-pilot, Alissa Davis, for helping me navigate across skies, seas and epochs, and for making sure Prehistoric Clock took all the time it needed..

Chapter One

Red Fire, White Steam, Blue Ocean

1908. Somewhere over the English Channel…

Verity collapsed her brass telescope and winced as the pyre of yet another British airship blazed on the rough waves. The odds of surviving this suicidal folly dwindled with each crimson flash. She shielded her face from the sting of lateral rain. All around her, metal warped and canvas groaned as the storm gathered fury. What she wouldn't give to be back in Angola right now, even in that godforsaken heat she was famous for griping about. Anywhere but here! Gusts battered the *Empress Matilda's* bullet-shaped, hydrogen-filled envelopes like a flurry of fists, swinging the deck and veering the airship away from the line of buoys below. Verity lurched against the taffrail, bit her tongue.

"Tangeni," she yelled for'ard through the pain.

Her stoic coxswain spun round. "Yes, *Eembu?*"

"Commence separation. Have Mbenga's team man the upper deck for you. Burton and Kwame can steer. Have Kibo meet me in the bell house." She clung to her sou'wester's chin strap with pruned fingers, and grinned bitterly. "It's time to divorce the *Empress.*"

Tangeni grimaced at their private joke, baring his too-many white teeth, and then shook his head. "English women crazier than English *men*."

"Oh, you haven't seen the half of it yet."

He snatched up the megaphone and bellowed orders to the crew. His oversized silver-blue slicker made him look like a fat sea lion leaning over the brass railing—a far cry from his hunting days in the wilds of Namibia.

A lull in the wind allowed her to dash safely to him across the poop deck. After placing her hands on his shoulders, they touched foreheads—perhaps for the last time. Her mission, they both knew, was now a halfpenny short of impossible. For years Tangeni had looked forward to seeing England for the first time. Only six miles shy, he would probably never be closer than he was right now.

The image of Captain Naismith hanging over the side amidships, burning to death in the steam jet from a ruptured boiler below as he reached for those poor drowning sailors, seized her heart. That was the moment she'd inherited this responsibility, this…countdown to oblivion.

"*Enda nawa,* Tangeni," she said. Regret ached through her shivering frame.

"Goodbye, *Eembu*."

As she hurried down the iron steps to the quarterdeck he called after her, "When rain stops, I buy us ice creams in Piccadilly."

The awful weight of finality squeezed the air from her lungs. Salutes from Reba and Philomena, the two statuesque Kenyan girls who maintained the balloons' canvas and lines, steeled her resolve, quickened her descent to B-deck. This crew was so far from home on a mission so alien to their lives in Africa, she at least owed it to them to give her very best, to reward their faith in English ingenuity. The admiralty's emergency telegram had snatched away their promised vacation and sped up their transfer to the London fleet—rotten enough circumstances for her first command *without* the threat of imminent death.

> BAC EMERGENCY ALERT STOP EMPRESS MATILDA PROCEED TO TRANS CHANNEL PIPELINE BUOYS SIXTY TO SEVENTY FIVE WITH UTMOST DISPATCH JOIN GANNET FLEET STOP OVER DOZEN ENEMY VESSELS SUNK OR SINKING BELIEVED TO CARRY FRAGILE FRZ THREE EXPLOSIVES EXTREME RISK TO PIPELINE STOP DEFUSE BOMBS AT ALL COSTS

At all costs? Those callous words hammered home as Verity ran to the square bell house in the centre of B deck, her heavy boots thumping across the wooden floor, then clanging on the riveted iron plates upon which the diving bell stood. At all costs? Granted, a rupture in the Dover-Calais petroleum pipeline would grind British industries to a halt for days, possibly weeks until it was repaired, but was that really more important than the lives of several good Gannet crews? Countless British Air Corps personnel had already drowned or been blown to bits tonight whilst trying to recover and defuse those enemy explosives safely aboard British vessels. The storm was simply too volatile, the waves too punishing for that kind of retrieval.

She had no choice but to take the fight to the sea bed.

Alone.

She remembered the words in her sister Bernie's final telegram from Angola, the last words she'd ever written before the rebel attack. "Come join me, sis. You will love it here, I promise." And in the top corner of the telegram, the ubiquitous British Steam Age motto stamped by the authorities, "Ambition Soars. The World Is Yours."

Bernie had believed utterly in the empire, and Father had given a proud, heartbreaking eulogy at her funeral. If those two people she'd always looked up to in her life reckoned the flag was worth dying for, if they measured humanity's progress with such sacrifice, who was Verity to argue? This was a vital mission. It was her chance to prove her worth to the cause.

No pressure, Verity. She eyed the diving bell's dull, copper curvature behind the square storehouse. *Literally, no pressure. Enjoy it while it lasts.*

Sea spray whipped through open seams all around as crewmen piled up from C-deck to help rotate the iron capstans fore and aft, cranking A-deck up to the clasps' tensile limits. As soon as the *Empress's* hull touched water, A-deck would lift free and Tangeni would try to fly it home through the storm, leaving the remainder of the vessel, a ship in its own right, to anchor to the buoy line and complete the mission. But so many things could go wrong with an uncoupling in *calm* weather, let alone in such an hellacious brew.

"*Eembu,* give me your hand," Kibo urged as he clung to the sturdy bell house rail. She gripped his arm just as the *Empress* thumped bow-first into the sea. The impact threw her against his broad shoulder, winding her. The capstan teams were floored like ten pins.

"Tell them to...hold steady...crank on my mark," Verity struggled between gasps. Kibo relayed her commands, held her while she doubled up to recover. *Christ,* of all the times to be winded...in the run-up to a crucial dive, when air meant everything.

The *Empress* listed dangerously to port. Howling gusts, yells and the sound of groaning metal filled B-deck. "Stop engine," she said. Now Tangeni had solo propulsion as well as lift—A-deck's propellers hummed faintly astern, above her. The vessel righted and she screamed to the signalman coordinating the two teams, "Lift her free!"

The heavy, zip-like *clak-clak-clak* of the rotating capstans quickened her pulse. She watched the signalman's tongue wag nervously in rhythm between his tight lips. A deafening clatter from every direction made her cover her ears. The iron clasps had uncoupled. When she looked up, the ceiling was alight. The dirigible banked away above, tilted to forty-five degrees by the strong wind, its propellers spitting streams of rain behind it.

The full weight of the storm heaped upon exposed B-deck.

"Kibo—" she now had to shout again through the fury, "—move those men from the capstans to the bell winch. As soon as I'm in, have them lift me over the side. You remember the drill?"

"Yes, *Eembu.* The captain went underwater plenty in the Indian Ocean. I oversaw all his dives."

"Good man. When I'm down there, you're captain here."

The big man's nose flared and his eyes bulged. He puffed his cheeks, saluted and then hurried aft, his familiar splay feet holding an amazingly straight line given the ship's tilt. Of all the officers on board, Verity had dealt with Kibo the least, as his duties tended to confine him to the steam engine rooms. His time spent maintaining and driving steam-powered automobile racers on the European circuits had inspired his brilliance in the ship's engine room. He had to dress the smartest—he wore a waistcoat at all times—and his subordinates had to be drilled to a level of efficiency unsurpassed in the fleet. Anything less and he would launch into his racing diatribes, and one might be forgiven for thinking he'd not only designed those cars, but invented steam locomotion as well.

Verity closed her eyes, prayed that he was as good as he boasted, then with her bell partner, Djimon, set about transferring diving gear from the storeroom to the diving bell. All too heavy, all too unwieldy—all indispensable. Only two other officers on board the *Empress Matilda* were qualified for both deep sea diving *and* defusing explosives. Captain Naismith was now dead, Tangeni airborne—but she would have volunteered anyway.

Father, Bernie and Britannia were watching over her.

But tonight, alas, Britannia did not rule the waves.

She pinched her nose and swallowed several times as the diving bell descended, its thick copper shell groaning. Her ears clicked, signalling she'd equalized the pressure. "Djimon, you're sure you know what to do?"

"Yes, *Eembu*. I haul you back up when you pull on lifeline."

"Exactly. But not too fast. I don't want the bends when I come up."

"Don't worry none, Lieutenant. I pull Captain Naismith up plenty times. He never gave cross word to Djimon. You in good hands."

Verity believed that about him, as she did about Kibo and Tangeni before him. These were some of the most capable men she'd ever met—diligent and unflappable in the line of duty. It steadied her nerves a little, knowing she had such strong arms waiting to pull her up if things should go pear-shaped. The confined space, too, helped focus her on the incremental suiting-up procedure she'd practised dozens of times, and away from the overwhelming odds of the mission.

She sucked in a crisp breath. Inside the greening copper sphere smelled of rubber and wet beach towels. She stripped to her white brassiere and tan jodhpurs, and Djimon helped her into her closed, waterproof rubber suit, the valves of which would let water out but not in. Heavy rubber bands sealed the suit at the wrists, leaving her hands free. She could barely move a step in her leaded diving boots, which weighed around thirty pounds, added to which Djimon fastened lead weights to her chest and back to maintain equilibrium. Lastly, he affixed the clunky metal helmet with side and front windows to the neck of her suit. It quickly grew warm inside, and her heavy breathing became the noise of her whole world. All told, she weighed more than her huge African partner. Even standing was exhausting.

She tapped her knuckles on the helmet, signalling for him to attach the non-collapsible umbilical. Air pumped through this hose would give her oxygen to breathe, as well as regulating the pressure inside the helmet, keeping the water level below her head. A much bigger hose from the *Empress* fed the diving bell in exactly the same way, ensuring seawater never rose above the moon pool—the open, central access point in the keel. If she or the bell tipped too far from the vertical, she would drown. If either pump stopped working, she would drown. Indeed, the thread of her existence underwater was so slender, so fragile that a few cubic inches of second-hand air were all that kept her alive by proxy.

Inches—inches versus an eternity of deep, dark unknown.

Djimon feverishly wound the dynamo handle and the hull lights blazed on, illuminating the moon pool to a turquoise hue. She sat on the brass rim and lowered her heavy boots into the freezing water. Clutching her umbilical, Djimon pretended to blow into it for her, a joke that gave her such levity before she sank, it almost made her cry. She patted the tool belt on her waist for good luck, nodded and slid into the Atlantic.

Cold seized and throbbed through her as though she had entered the liquid heart of a glacier. Directly below, tall, wispy green stems drooped over a bed of murky sand. The bell's lights revealed the wreckage of a medium-sized coalition freighter a short distance ahead, mere yards from the large black pipeline. A crew of thirty to forty enemy souls had been lost here—terrorists smuggling explosives into England, yes, but still a terrible waste of life. She shuddered. Her fingertips tingled icily. But Kibo's undersea lookouts had done well to pinpoint this site for her, and he had anchored the *Empress* to the correct buoy cable. Now it was all up to her.

Ice creams on Piccadilly, she recalled Tangeni's parting words. *Easy does it.*

Her boots gently touched the bottom. The suit's top-heaviness gave her forward momentum as she leaned. Her clumsy steps formed an ungainly trudge but she didn't care. Her every breath amplified to a gasp inside the helmet but the rhythm kept her company. She reached the mangled brass bulwark and walked around it, mindful to keep her hose from snagging on a jutting end. Through her right window she glimpsed a tiny crimson flash. Moments later, a school of eel-like fish darted across her path and sand fidgeted all about, as though a distant but powerful impact had rippled the ocean bed.

Verity swallowed hard. A bomb had to have just exploded somewhere close to the pipeline. Had a BAC officer, just like her, been blown to bits while trying to defuse it? Too late to back out now. She looked up. The black cylinder stretched deep into the gloom on either side. Unmoved, assimilated by weeds and crustaceans, it resembled the charred remains of some colossal leviathan skeleton from ancient times. *A kraken...which must not be cracked.* Thank God her reliable bad puns were still intact.

She located the aft hold, partially collapsed, and crept through the splintered iron hatch. It was too dark inside, so she lit a flare from her tool belt and dropped it at the hatchway. Rose light flooded the hold, skewing the shadows of strewn boxes against buckled walls. In the middle of the floor, a shiny silver-and-black clarinet lay untouched. The last object she'd expected to find there. Silver bubbles from her valves collected on the sloping

13

roof and rolled above a stack of long metal boxes marked *EXPLOSIVO*.

Christ. There were at least six boxes! FRZ-3 clockwork explosives were not difficult to defuse—the detonating coil could be removed with a screwdriver and a portable oxyacetylene cutter, both of which she had in her belt—but the explosive material itself was quite unstable. A heavy blow to any FRZ-3 bomb would explode it without the need for a detonator. Therefore she must be careful not to let anything hit the device or—*God forbid*—let one of the boxes spill.

She unfastened the cords holding the boxes in place and carefully, one at a time, lowered the five-foot-long containers flat onto the floor. Her pruned fingers shivered but the operation was well within her capabilities. She'd performed this job countless times on ships and in shallow water, usually on redundant British mines. Time, rather than difficulty, was now her biggest concern. Every minute she spent underwater prolonged the time she would have to decompress in the bell later on. If she were to surface too quickly, the gases in her bloodstream might create a dangerous, perhaps fatal bubble—an air embolism.

But she would have to take her chan—

The entire hold shook. A deep, twisting grind felt like something was tunnelling up through the iron wreck. She gazed up in horror as several rivets shot loose from the ceiling, allowing her bubbles to squirm through a gap. The metal began to warp inward, downward…onto the explosives!

A tremendous weight pressed the iron panels. She stumbled sideways over a fallen crate. Seawater gushed up her nose, making her cough. She righted herself instantly in mid-fall but lost her bearings. Still the ceiling warped, lower and lower. A few more feet and she'd be a memory.

Think, Verity, think. How can you save yourself and *the pipeline? You can't defuse the bombs now. Not here. What about—*

That was it! She dragged the boxes out through the hatchway one at a time, barely sliding the last one away before the full weight of a huge steam funnel rent the iron apart. It crushed the hold completely.

The enormity of her narrow escape seeped in. She panted and watched a cloud of white smoke rise from the split funnel and envelop the black pipeline. It could so easily have been the shock heard throughout the empire. Major damage to the industries. The end of Verity Champlain. For some reason, the latter struck her as being the less important of the two. *Why is that?* She didn't want to die. So what the deuce was she *doing* here, a martyr to deep sea petroleum? And why hadn't that occurred to her before? The notion gouged a chilling void in the pit of her stomach. What insane confluence of events had led her to this spot? What destiny? Orders? She frowned and tugged a slimy stem of sea grass free from its roots in the sand.

A twitch on the slenderest thread of life had almost brought her whole world crashing down, and for what?

Maybe it was the pressure talking.

After blinking sweat from her eyes, Verity dragged the boxes to a safe distance and defused the hexagonal clockwork explosives in the bell's light. She had to leave one, however, as her cutter ran out of acetylene. Instead she buried it in the sand at a safe distance from the pipeline, and then made her way back to the diving bell.

One hard tug on her lifeline was all the signal Djimon needed to haul her slowly up. As she rose, several more crimson flashes lit the distant gloom.

She blew damp strands out of her eyes, then heaved a sigh. What had *other* crews gone through in the name of Britannia tonight?

Chapter 2

Son of a Marquess

"Get out of my way, blue bottle." Lord Garrett Embrey brushed the irritating old butler aside and marched along the strip of tan carpet flanked by varnished oak panels. Too many nautical oil paintings adorned the corridor walls. Grosvenor House was as self-righteously appointed as its committee members, and he'd long grown tired of this superciliousness.

"May I take your hat and coat, My Lord?" The pesky servant wearing a shiny blue waistcoat scurried after him.

Embrey stopped outside the new conference room door, inhaled the strong smell of lacquer and then shrugged his damp top coat off while the man held it for him. He handed his top hat behind him and waited until the blue bottle's shoes squeaked away out of earshot. This moment to gather himself before the interrogation was the most crucial time of the evening, he knew. He plucked his father's bronze pocketwatch inscribed with the Embrey coat-of-arms from his waistcoat—the timepiece was pretty much the only item belonging to the old man he still used—and raised an eyebrow.

Seven-twenty-five. He was deliciously late.

Oh, let them slither a while longer.

The 1801 Thomas Luny painting, *Battle of the Nile*, caught his eye. Thrilling and majestic, it echoed the nautical reminiscences his father had shared with him by the fireside after many a dinner. As far back as he could recall, Garrett had loved imagining them perched together in the crow's nest of a grand ship of the line, sharing a spyglass in the run-up to a fierce engagement. How often he'd pictured his older self as the spitting image of Marquess Embrey, a much-admired figure in London society. Alas, how little he resembled his father these days! In his teens, everyone had remarked on the likeness. Now at twenty-five, Garrett was a little over six feet tall, broad-shouldered, strikingly blond, and he had his mother's sharply defined, heart-shaped face that many had called handsome. But it was in his father's name that he must contend with the Special Committee on War Crimes this evening.

Eighteen months after they had wrongfully convicted and executed Marquess Embrey for treachery against the Crown, the vipers still wanted more blood. Now they were after *him,* the last surviving member of one of the oldest aristocratic families in England. He tempered his urge to punch a hole through the glass by loosening his shoulders as he would on the playing fields of Oxford. He straightened his white bow tie and winged collar. During this meeting, his rage would have to remain subcutaneous, for his enemies were circling, and he must not be baited.

Very well—have at it, vipers.

He flung the door open and a score of gazes tried to strip him bare. Two long mahogany tables formed a V in the middle of a vast maroon carpet. The low ceiling, the centric lighting and the broad dimensions of the room had been designed to intimidate, to set visitors immediately ill-at-ease.

The game was afoot.

As he had during his Oxford days, Embrey fed off the challenge. He'd sparred with Sir Horace Holly himself on the debating floor, and the old adventurer had personally lauded his composure. It would take more than legal double-talk to ruffle him. He breezed to his chair held out for him by a gaunt, monocled clerk, bowed to the vipers slithering to their places, and sat.

"Lord Embrey, might we enquire as to the reason for your tardiness? I recall this is not the first time." The hawkish, crookbacked chairman, the Rt. Hon. Lorne Wallingford, a member of the Whig cabinet, didn't look up from the documents arrayed in front of him.

"You may enquire, yes."

"I see. And may we now also proceed, if Your Lordship deigns to stand accused?"

Hateful old Quasimodo. "Pray proceed, sir, if you have the gall to accuse face-to-face."

"Very well. Let us begin," Crookback said, to much rustling of paper around the tables. "On March seventh last year, your father, the Marquess of Embrey, and your uncle, Lord Fitzwalter, were executed after being found guilty of treason against the Crown. Their crimes were perpetrated in the Benguela region of Angola, West Africa, and those actions led to a vicious assault by our enemies on the construction of our second Leviacrum tower—an assault which, I must remind you, cost the lives of hundreds of British servicemen and women. Lord Embrey, you have been summoned by this committee to answer the charge of aiding that assault by means of direct correspondence with your father and

19

uncle, assisting in the redeployment of British regiments from Benguela, and by contacting elements of the rebel Coalition forces *personally*."

Embrey shot out of his seat at that last remark. "*What?* Since when? What *is* this? I demand an explanation." Hushed chatter throughout the assembly suggested this was a pre-emptive gambit, something Wallingford and his cronies had cooked up in private. In other words, a hatchet job. Remembering his promise to keep his composure was the only thing stopping him from chinning the old bastard, crookbacked or not.

"I have before me signed documents proving your collusion, sir. No further explanation is needed. Professors Talbot and Vaughn-Britton, two noted forensic document examiners, are willing to testify under oath that it is indeed your signature. They are waiting in the next room. I will summon them in due course, but first I would like to read the documents aloud to this committee so that it might better gauge the gravity of your complicity in these events."

Embrey thrust an adamant finger at the chairman. "You dare spit one more word of fiction. I'm warning you."

Forged letters? Handwriting experts? Throwing an insane charge of treason at him? It was so eerily reminiscent of Father's and Uncle Ralph's travesty of a trial at the Old Bailey that he shuddered. His knuckles and fingertips gripping the table's edge turned white. He lifted them and watched his moist fingerprints fade to darkness. Would his family name, his great and noble lineage, be next? He stepped to one side. An atavistic call to flight rang through him from head to toe—it urged him to take the quickest possible exit.

"Lord Embrey, the sooner you take your seat and cooperate, the sooner you will have your opportunity to rebut these charges. Bear in mind, sir, that this is only a preliminary hearing and no official criminal indictments have entered the judiciary. Our job is merely to ascertain the veracity of these documents…and your own evidence, of course." Crookback leaned across to confer with his colleague, a much taller, fat man with a double chin.

How did these sons of bitches get *away* with stunts like this? Embrey stepped farther from his chair.

"Lord Embrey," Double Chin said, "I must remind you that until these hearings are satisfactorily resolved, you must not leave London."

"Who put you up to this? The Leviacrum Council?"

"I beg your pardon!"

"You'll rot in hell for this. Mark my words, *you unconscionable bastards.*" Embrey thumped the table with a livid fist. So much for composure.

Crookback whispered something to the monocled clerk, who rushed for the door Embrey had entered through. This couldn't end well. Two police constables guarded the front of Grosvenor House, and Wallingford was clearly after apprehending him here and now. Those forged letters were as good as arrest warrants.

The urge to flee stiffened his considerable frame. But through one door waited the police, and through the other…learned forensic stooges ready to tighten the noose and sell their souls to the hot place.

"Might I at least see these letters first?" He stalked behind the line of swivelling snakes and toward the brain of this political Hydra—old Crookback himself. "For all

I know, you mistook my signature for my father's." Those words choked him but he carried on.

Wallingford kept a defiant expression, adjusted his pince-nez as Embrey approached. "Nonsense. They have been thoroughly—"

Embrey barged him sideways off his chair. The old crookback squealed and hit the carpet with a thud. Protestations erupted all around the "V" but Embrey kept his composure when it mattered, just as he'd promised. He stuffed the folder containing the forged letters inside his waistcoat, and bolted for the clerk's chair which stood beneath one of the arched windows.

Double Chin accosted him from behind. "Blackguard! Traitor! You won't get away that easily!"

Incensed, Embrey reached inside his tail coat with both hands and drew two steam-pistols from the clip-on holsters over his hips. He thrust them in Double Chin's beetroot face. "Step away, you sack of shit."

The man spun and waddled after his fleeing colleagues with surprising speed. Embrey holstered his sidearms and then hurled the chair through the window. The clatter of glass merged with the thunder of heavy rain outside. A formidable gust flung both shards and stinging water at him. He ducked.

"Stay where you are. This is the police!"

Jesus. Embrey glanced over his shoulder as the constables charged across the empty conference room waving truncheons. He vaulted onto the stone window sill, then leapt out onto the privet hedge. It broke his fall nicely. After clambering over an iron fence with arrow-tipped posts, he sprinted down Hendron Street with only one thing on his mind…

Leaving England—as soon as possible.

The chimes of Big Ben barely registered through the torrential downpour. Eight o'clock and still he ran. The Chamber of Commerce, the Westminster Observatory, and even the row of giant dirigible hangars lining the Thames were deserted as he passed. Over a mile behind, high up in the storm clouds, the lighthouse atop the Leviacrum flashed brilliantly, guiding wayward airships home through the treacherous weather. Such a laudable beacon, yet the giant tower was far more than an aviation aid. Many of the country's brightest minds gathered there to research, to confer and to implement scientific breakthroughs. This controlled explosion of ingenuity had heralded a new age for British supremacy around the globe. But why did the Leviacrum have to grow taller every year? The cylindrical copper and iron edifice already reached thousands of feet high, and still the Council insisted on its upward expansion. Some said it would one day pierce space itself. That may have been the plan all along.

But why? And for the love of God, why build another one thousands of miles away on an African plateau? The official reason—that Britain needed a fortified headquarters to coordinate the extraction of natural resources from that region—had rung false to Father and Uncle Ralph for years, and it rang false to him now. Digging for petroleum, gold, copper, iron and diamonds had nothing at all to do with building a skyscraping edifice. And what *was* it about his family that frightened the Leviacrum Council so much? Before the arrests, he'd had no warning, no inkling that his world would be flipped upside down.

What secret had Father uncovered during his expedition to the Benguela Plateau?

The wet cobbled road suddenly blazed with yellow light. Embrey spun. The blinding headlights of an automobile bounced after him. He skipped onto the pavement, rested against a streetlamp and retrieved the folder from his waistcoat. He pretended to read it under the breast of his coat as though it was a map and he was lost in the rain. Police couldn't afford steam-powered vehicles, so it had to be a civilian. The driver might stop and offer him a lift. If not, at the very least, no one would suspect him of running for his life.

The brass car clattered by; the moustached driver didn't even notice him. Typical steamhead—always in a hurry, cocooned in his contraption. Embrey walked after it at a breezy pace along Whitehall and Parliament Street, reckoning it would take him another twenty minutes or so to reach Jack Sorkin's marina on foot. His yacht, the *Lady Godiva,* was berthed there, and he had enough provisions aboard to last him across the channel to France. The crossing might be deuced dangerous in a storm but he would not last long on the run in London. He could always hug the coast until the weather subsided. His whole world seemed to be flying apart on the vicious gusts, washing away in the gutter torrents. How could something like this *happen* to the son of a marquess, a peer of the realm?

What would the boys at the social club make of all this?

He stopped dead. The faint *clack-clack* of horses' hooves on the cobbles froze his blood and he immediately reached for his pistols. *No,* it might not be the police. He'd be calling unnecessary attention to himself if he drew on an innocent coachman. But what kind of coach would be out in this weather? The storm had now raged for two hours, at least. He glanced to his right…

…and bolted at the sight of four Black Marias hurtling down Bridge Street.

He passed Westminster station on his left and spied the turn for the Victoria Embankment ahead. Not enough time. Good athlete though he was, he was fagged, and the police had clocked him. Their clattering pursuit gained ground.

God Almighty.

An ungainly-looking vehicle rolled out of the rain sheets ahead. It resembled a small, steam-powered tractor with only three wheels, and pulled a white carriage behind it. It moved at a fair speed and had just crossed Westminster Bridge. Embrey drew his pistols, bid the driver stop.

"Oi, what's *your* game?" the Manchester man protested. He wore a flat cap and a white milkman's jacket. A young boy cowered in the passenger seat. "Don't 'urt us, mister. We sell ice cream, that's all."

"I don't have time to explain. Turn onto Victoria Embankment *right now*." Embrey wrenched the stiff door open and climbed in, shuffling the boy up against his father. "Go as fast as you can."

Despite his terrified expression, the man reached for the valve handle and pressed it slowly forward, precipitating a gentle *hiss,* then a *clunk, clunk* as the vehicle gathered steam. It accelerated quickly as he turned the wheel.

"Head up the embankment. See if you can make it to Wharf Fourteen."

"The *Griffin*?"

"Indeed. Can't this heap go any faster?"

"Jus' let 'er catch 'er breath first," the man boasted, but the Marias hurtled into view before he completed the turn.

"Oh, Christ." Embrey hurriedly removed the propulsion cylinders from his pistols, felt their weight. Good—plenty of acid and water to combine and create steam pressure for both weapons. He reaffixed them. The gap-toothed young boy clung to his father's jacket, eyeing Embrey with what appeared equal parts fear and fascination. Clutched under the lad's arm was a thin, cloth-bound book. "Don't worry, chief. These aren't for you." Embrey clinked the brass weapons together.

"Daddy, what's 'appened to the rain?" the lad called out.

Embrey looked up. *What the deuce…?* The rain had taken on a lilac luminosity, as though bathed in some kind of purple light. But light from where? He scrutinized the nearest factory. One or two oil lamps glowed inside, nothing untoward. The boy and his father scanned the river and the sky, each turning back to Embrey with blank expressions. Now the rain appeared to fizz as it fell, emitting acidic smoke on the ground. A loud sizzling all about made him fear the vehicle itself might be in danger.

The entire riverside seemed to be cooking with liquid brimstone.

The boy hid his face behind the book as a blinding purple flash forced his father to swerve…

Chapter 3

The Clockwatcher

The tiny house spider scurried out onto the brass pipe moments before steam hissed from a nearby valve. The factory's heating system was starting its evening cycle. Cecil, slouched sideways in his chair, chin on palm, shifted his elbow from the chair arm to the warm pipe. How long could he keep it there before the heat grew too intense? Who would move first, him or the trapped spider? Could he *be* any more neurotic tonight?

Traces of the Leviacrum representative's African lily perfume lingered on his gangway overlooking the giant, restless machine. Miss Polperro and her dozen cronies were busy inspecting it below, making notes…assessing his progress for the Council. Jackals! They had their agenda, he had his. What gave them the right to scrutinize his experiment when their own skyscraping venture remained the empire's most closely guarded secret?

Well, two can play at that game.

He stood his hinged, twin picture frames beside him on the fold-up metal table and tilted the photographs toward him. He hadn't wanted the Leviacrum spies to see how personal this experiment was to him, or that this spot on the gangway was his favourite place in the world. Lisa's timid smile and distant, ethereal eyes belonged up here with him. Their black-and-whiteness did not register. Through his spectrometer goggles he saw only full colour—her flush cheeks, hazel eyes and beautiful auburn hair. Little Edmond's curious intellect almost leapt out of the frame. Cecil smiled, shifted his goggle lens to a higher magnification. The boy had his features alright: black curly hair, a thin face with a square chin and that famous Reardon button nose, eyes a little too close together. Edmond might have grown up bookish and odd-looking like his dad but he'd also had his mother's sweet and sensitive nature. Under her tutelage he would have become a good, moral man, a man with many friends. What would he have made of his father's reclusive quest—this epically selfish machine?

Would either of them approve of him unravelling time to bring them back? Perhaps messing up the temporal works for good? He'd asked their images a thousand times and his heart's response had never wavered, not in six years.

Do everything within your power. Nothing else matters. You will never be complete if you don't try. Let God stop it if He must.

The massive primary brass cogs flanking the machine lurched incrementally forward, powering the network of gears and pistons. He'd designed the machine in a creative fever six years ago, shortly after quitting his job as laboratory supervisor in the Leviacrum. His work there had concerned the acceleration of psammeticum energy in subspace lens refraction, specifically to send light waves a tenth of a second back or forward through time.

He had achieved both those goals, but despite unlimited resources, the Leviacrum scientists had not made further progress since his departure. A tenth of a second, on such a small scale, had no practical use. These spies had come to check on his progress because their research had hit a brick wall. They were desperate for a breakthrough.

Little did they know he'd been on the verge of that breakthrough for the past four years.

His machine rolled cosmic dice continually, once every ten seconds, every hour of every day. He leaned over the brass railing and inhaled the delicious smell of petroleum and steam, his favourite combination anywhere on Earth apart from the scent of African lily, Lisa's perfume.

He flinched as the house spider scurried along his arm. *Well, well.* The critter had outwitted him, escaped the hot pipe by using its opponent, Cecil—swapping one danger for another. The lesser of two evils. Nature's own difference engine at work? The parallel for his own plight tickled him, and he caged the spider in his fingers and lowered it onto the gridiron gangway, then watched it scurry away to safety.

"Professor Reardon, I have one last question for you." The insufferable woman's footsteps rattled the platform behind him.

He turned and cupped a hand over his ear, pretending he hadn't heard. How dare these jackals yell at him in his own factory.

She approached, wiping the moisture from her thick-rimmed spectacles. The hem of her grey walking suit snagged on a jutting end of steel and ripped. Cecil bit his lip to hide his amusement.

"Everything seems in order." Miss Polperro freed her skirt and then tapped her pencil on her clipboard. "We are most impressed with your psammeticum transfer process—very novel. But my colleagues and I are unable to discern the precise mechanism calculating the angles and indices of refraction. All we can find is a Hillary magno-abacus, hardly an advancement. Is that the hub of your machine?" Disdain poured from her snooty remarks, as though she regarded him as a pesky insect to be stepped on, and she'd wasted her time even coming here.

Exactly the reaction he'd hoped for.

"Yes, the abacus is calculating those measurements," he lied.

"Modified of course?"

Uh-oh. Best not make it too obvious. "Yes, greatly modified. But Hillary's design was always the best template."

The corner of her thin lips curled cruelly, precipitating an unpleasant levity across her schoolmarm face. "Indeed. Thank you for your time, Professor. I will make my report to the Council first thing tomorrow. The next inspection is scheduled for six months from now. Oh yes, have you any questions for us?"

Only a trillion that you'll never answer. "No. I believe this concludes our business for now. Good evening, Miss Polperro." He waved to the throng of shadowy cronies huddled together near the spiral stairwell.

"Good evening." She handed him a copy of the full disclosure document he'd signed earlier. It stated that he was still bound by the Official Leviacrum Secrecies Act, and that if he withheld any new scientific discoveries based upon his work in said institution, he faced prosecution and a potential charge of treason against the Crown.

Familiar threats were bandied about indiscriminately in England these days. As soon as the jackals had left, he screwed the document into a cricket ball and bowled it over-arm into the molten iron furnace a hundred feet below—that section of his factory he leased as a miniature steelworks to a new Irish company. "*How's that?*" he mimicked the fielding team's reaction to a wicket keeper's catch. He'd loved cricket once upon a time, and Lisa had loved to watch him play…

His tightening fists squeaked on the moist brass railing.

How one skidding automobile, barely out of arm's reach, could destroy a man's life so completely. The sting of ice pellets thrown up by the crash, the way Lisa had contorted her slender frame in an attempt to shield Edmond, the unimaginable helplessness he'd felt as he'd watched on, frozen, impotent. No, he daren't dissect the memory any more, not when he was so close to erasing it forever. He hissed and shook his head, trying to loosen the memory but it was lodged. Cecil Reardon, husband and father? Tail coat and top hat in the morning, pyjamas and dinner jacket in the afternoon and for interminable months afterward…

His lips receded from his teeth. The molten metal in the vat below ran through his veins tonight. He'd just lied to the Leviacrum Council, staked his fortune and his life on a roll of the dice that might never come to pass.

But the device at the heart of his difference engine held more than just promise. It was destined, a family affair. He'd fashioned it after his famous ancestor's blueprints for a celestial chronometer. John Harrison had invented the first accurate seafaring chronometers used by the British Navy in the late eighteenth century. Yet, unbeknownst to the public, he had also drawn up plans for a timepiece so accurate, so versatile, it could be adapted into a difference engine of mind-boggling application.

Cecil had achieved that and more besides. And the world's first steam-powered temporal differentiator ticked away beneath him, the numbers on its brass dials hidden from official science like the invisible countdown of life was hidden from all living things. For now, God alone was privy to the correct sequence that would turn back history to before the crash. But finding those numbers, he knew, was only a matter of time.

He sat once more on his chair on the gangway and crossed his legs. How many days and nights had he waited here, watched over the instrument of his salvation? The hissing, whirring, clanking brain below seemed to speak to him. It said, "Everything within our power. Let God stop us if He must."

Minutes passed like hours. He'd begun to nod off when a noxious fizz in the air made him cough. He eased to his feet and scowled at a strange lilac light seeping up through the steam like luminous grains in an upside-down hourglass. His pulse outpaced the machine's rhythm for the first time in weeks. The light appeared to have emerged from…*the Harrison clock?* The only thing he could think of was to get to his differentiator and record the numbers. Something truly extraordinary had happened inside his machine, and he needed to know when and why.

In moments, the entire factory glowed with lilac webbing on the walls and rain that fizzed, burned on his skin. He pulled his dinner jacket over his head and rushed for the stairwell, never more frightened or excited in his life.

Before he left the gangway, a blinding purple flash blazed throughout the factory…

Chapter 4

Homecoming

The propellers' waspish drone comforted her like a familiar voice through the tumult outside. Kibo had suggested she rest awhile in his quarters at the rear of B-deck, as hers had flooded during the sea landing and the captain's cabin had not yet been cleared. His bed was as neat and clean as his reputation suggested. Funny really, through the night's chaos and the shocking loss of life on and below the raging Atlantic, how anything could remain so dry, so hospitable. She folded her arms under her head on the pillow and tried to make sense of the maelstrom of events. Bursts of apocalyptic imagery blazed in her mind's eye: the exploding hydrogen envelopes of nearby airships, the decks capsizing in a sea-ring of orange flames, those underwater crimson flashes detonating in clusters like popping frog spawn. How many bombs had been set off, how many divers killed, how many crews lost in that concerted suicide mission?

It would take more time and distance to properly digest her part in the worst calamity ever suffered by the Gannet fleet. At least, according to initial reports, the pipeline had not been breached. And at least they had made it safely to the Dover amphibian hangar, along with Tangeni and his dirigible section. She heaved a sigh of relief for that. Her first officer had proven himself a formidable airship navigator. Their two halves of the *Empress Matilda* now reattached—the Dover crane crews were amazingly proficient compared with their colonial counterparts in Africa—Verity was making for the Gannet hangar on the bank of the Thames. The poor Dover boys had enough damaged craft to contend with. Relatively unscathed, the *Matilda* was ready for redeployment as soon as another crew could be found.

"Feeling any warmer, *Eembu*?" Tangeni stood dripping wet at the door.

"A little. I need to soak in a hot bath for a week, though."

"This might help in the meantime." He handed her a hot water bottle, then draped a second blanket over her. "Lieutenant Champlain, now Captain Champlain. You did amazing things tonight."

"Thank you, and so did you. But it doesn't feel like much of an accomplishment, not when all those other crews—God, there were so *many*—"

"Yes, but *Eembu* is not responsible for other crews. *Empress Matilda* performed her service with great aplomb—" she loved his ever-expanding vocabulary, "—and we are all still here because English women crazier than English men. In war, crazy always wins."

"You think I'm crazy, Tangeni?" The notion rang eerily true, for she'd already confronted it during her underwater ordeal.

He shrugged and cast her a wide-eyed, questing gaze. "Sometimes crazy means not blinking. English are famous for not blinking in the face of enemies. So are Ovambo," he said proudly. Then he rolled his eyes.

"And who would fly on a balloon boat who *wasn't*...how do you say...pots-for-rags?" Another English colloquialism he'd picked up, probably from her. She laughed out loud, exciting her tickly cough.

A junior crewman ran up to him. "Lieutenant Tangeni, come quick. Leviacrum tower is hailing us."

Tangeni nodded and turned to leave. "Let me know if it's anything urgent," she reminded him.

"Yes, ma'am."

Through her porthole window, sheets of rain wavered over the gloomy city. Of the large, silhouetted buildings lining the riverfront, she first recognised the Westminster Observatory's copper dome. Verity hadn't seen London for over four years, but drifting toward Westminster, the heart of British regency, filled her with quiet awe. A patriotic swell she hadn't experienced since Bernie's funeral ached in her temples and behind her eyes.

The Houses of Parliament were deserted and only streetlamps illuminating rain-minted patches of road suggested life continued in the capital. She sighed, flipped onto her side to savour the view, and clutched the hot water bottle between her thighs. A flash of lightning lit Big Ben's clock face. Only five past eight? The day had been dark for an eternity. She wondered if Aunt Jemima would still be awake when Verity reached her house on Challenger Row. Uncle Stephen probably would be—he usually smoked himself into a daze until the early hours. She snuggled into the glad memories. Safe eccentricities in a household where nothing ever seemed to change—that was the tonic she needed after a night like tonight.

The *Empress* lost a little altitude, drifted toward the embankment. It must be a strong wind veering her off course. Tangeni would compensate.

What on earth...?

After rubbing her eyes, she sat up and gazed at the factory next to the station house across the road from Big Ben. A peculiar lilac glow emanated from its roof and appeared to column—no, to mushroom—out into the night. Her heavy chest began to drum when the rain outside her window snaked, fizzed like streams of acid confetti. She could no longer see the shape of the lilac mushroom, which meant...

...the *Empress* must be *inside it?*

She leapt out of bed in the spare midshipman's uniform Kibo had lent her, and sprinted across B-deck. The awestruck crewmen and women gathered at the windows, mesmerised. One or two ran after her, conversing worriedly in their native tongues. By the time she reached A-deck, the airship flew so low it was heading straight for Westminster Bridge! Tangeni yelled for Reba and Philomena to empty the port and starboard ballast tanks, but the ship was too low—it would not lift clear in time.

"Forget that," Verity yelled. "Turn her completely around. Full starboard engines."

Tangeni relayed the command, adding something terse in Ovambo. He removed his slicker and threw it around Verity's shoulders. She shrugged it off—the ship wasn't going to turn in time either. "Emergency separation *now,*" she cried. "It's our only—"

The night and London vanished in a brilliant purple flash. She blinked and rubbed her eyes furiously. The *Empress* plummeted as though her balloons had cut loose. Verity's stomach leapt into her throat. But the separation couldn't have caused this—she was on A-deck.

The hull splashed down with a *thump* that threw her onto her back. Her head smacked the deck. After a few seconds, the *Empress's* taut rigging and bullet-shaped, dark blue envelopes scrawled back into vision and she frowned. For instead of storm clouds, a bright turquoise light filled the sky. Yet thunder growled all about. She had to squint to adjust to what appeared a cloudless summer's day, but it was no use. Her crown throbbed, sending her further and further into a daze. The *Empress* groaned and listed badly to starboard. The last thing she saw before blacking out was the skewed edifice of Big Ben.

It appeared to have been sliced in half, vertically.

Chapter 5

Last Chimes of Big Ben

A ten-foot surge of Thames water swept the getaway car onto its side, crashing it through the factory's wire-mesh fence. Freezing water gushed over Embrey from the driver's shattered window and kept piling in. Trapped between his buckled door and the twisted brass dash, he struggled to crouch upright until his forearms and hip bled. No use. The water level rose to his chin but he could not budge. Red drops peppered his face…

Above him, a tiny limb stirred from beneath the driver's shredded white coat. The crash had hurled the man part-way through the windscreen, cutting him to ribbons. Trembling fingers pushed their way between his thigh and the broken seat. The driver's body flopped loose, now hanging only by glass edges skewering his chest and neck.

"Boy, I need your help," Embrey said. "I know you don't want to, but listen… *Look at me*. I'm drowning. I have moments left."

The youngster gibbered half syllables and gazed at Embrey with eyes the size of saucers. He shook his head.

"It's all right, son. I'm frightened too. But if you help me out this once, I promise I'll put everything right."

God forgive me. "Those steam-pistols I showed you—one of them is lodged right here under my leg. I can't reach it. It's loaded and I need you to fetch it and shoot out the window. Can you do that for me?" The lad clung to his dead father's trouser legs, quivering, not crying. "What's your name, chief?"

No response. Still the Thames water trickled in, and Embrey raised his mouth another inch, barely above it. "You sell ice creams with your father? Well, my daughter loves ice creams. If you don't fetch my gun *right now,* she's never going to see me again. Son, *I'm going to die.* I've got one breath left. If you don't help me by the time it runs out, I'll be dead. And you'll have—" No, he couldn't lay that on the boy. "Look at me, son. Look—"

His elbow slipped and he went under before he'd saved a breath. *Oh, Christ, please don't let this be the end. I'm not ready—*

A deep rumble, dark slipstreams and the rush of bubbles up his nostrils answered his prayer. The boy rummaged frantically underwater. His boots whacked Embrey's chin again and again, making him grimace. Embrey knew his lungs held reserves of oxygen beyond his brain's estimation, but not much. On the verge of panic, he shut his eyes and focused on the reflection he'd seen in the painting earlier that evening. He was the son of a proud and noble family. He had his mother's looks and his father's stubborn resolve. The might of the empire wanted him dead but…the young son of an ice-cream seller would get to make that call. A broiling anti-breath choked him from inside. It thickened like soot clogging a chimney. The bitter temptation to breathe water for the first time since the womb subsumed him and spread wide. He gave a silent scream.

A muffled *thud* answered.

The water emptied from the car in moments as if it had been sucked out. Embrey gasped for life and found that he could move freely. The shattered window had released the twisted dash from his hip. He coughed until his heart burned, then he slowly crawled free from the wreckage.

It was a brilliant summer's day...in a world he no longer recognised.

The boy scampered out after him, thrusting the steam-pistol hither and thither as ungodly sounds haunted the derelict remains of Whitehall and Westminster. Embrey pried the gun from the lad's hands, scooped him up and held him tight. "I've got you, chief. Don't worry, I've got you. It's all over now. We're safe, you and I. Safe as can be." The boy clung to his neck, sobbing.

They were standing at the epicentre of a cataclysmic event. For roughly two hundred yards ahead and to his left, London appeared more or less as it should be, geographically. Westminster station house, the gentleman's club behind that, the row of factories lining Victoria Embankment—all had partially collapsed but were at least recognisable. Behind him to the south, across Bridge Street, filthy Thames water swamped Speaker's Green at the foot of Big Ben, while the rear section of the clock tower itself appeared to be missing! Its roof and spire had crumbled away and it was a miracle the edifice stood at all. Worse still, Westminster Palace had vanished completely. In its place, a fifty-foot-wide gorge swallowed the last of the Thames-that-was.

To his right, Westminster Pier and a fraction of Westminster Bridge were raised against a shallow rocky

41

escarpment. A crashed airship lay listed to one side against Victoria Embankment, its two giant blue, bullet-shaped balloons trying to tug it upright. Beyond the bounds of this city slice, grassland and a peculiar forest formed a kind of circumjacent barrier, about three miles in diameter, from the rest of the world. The only gap in the tree line occurred beyond the airship to the north-east, where the escarpment fell away to a sloping valley. As his nostrils cleared, Embrey reckoned he could smell a strange sea air.

He put the boy down while he took off his tail coat and threw it over the poor driver's lacerated body. The lad shouldn't have to see that. He hooked his arm around the youngster as they walked back toward Bridge Street, where a half dozen policeman and horses—his pursuers—lay crushed under rubble from the collapsed station house wall. Distant shouts and screams seemed to be coming from the ruins beyond. Though his brow and hip were cut and his clothes sopping, there might be others in far worse shape, trapped, in need of rescue. He would do all he could.

"W-where are we?" the boy murmured.

"I don't know, chief. I just…don't know. But wherever it is, it ain't quite London."

While he traversed Bridge Street, wandering through a mist no doubt caused by the sudden meeting of cold and warm air from different times, theories explaining this startling phenomenon jostled in his mind. Rumblings of advanced science, no, *meta*-science being enacted in the Leviacrum tower had been rife since he was a boy. Scaremongering, he'd always thought. The tabloids and penny dreadfuls had so exhaustively exploited those rumours for ghoulish readers that the ideas themselves—reanimating corpses, the hybridization of man and animal species, eternal youth, invisibility—had long become jaded urban myths. No one took them for real any more than they did the gods of Mount Olympus.

Yet, at least *one* of them had just reached forth from the margins of cheap fiction and, without warning, smote the doubting heart of London.

Time travel.

As a concept, it was quickly out of the regular man's grasp.

But it was here now, a force as real as gravity, and he'd better start getting to grips with it if he had any hope of solving this shocking turn of events.

Was this a freak accident? Or had someone, somewhere managed to deduce the physical science behind time travel, that elusive action hitherto confined to dreams and the recalling of memories? Someone from the Leviacrum? The lilac explosion had mushroomed from the riverside factory. Was that some secret test facility licenced by the Council? And this horrific transplanting of Westminster and Whitehall was the collateral damage from some official experiment gone awry? This *reeked* of Leviacrum scientific meddling. Umpteen airship crashes over the years had been traced back to their reckless prototype innovations, including the big crash of '98, which had partly demolished Buckingham Palace. Then there was the lunar rocket debacle of '03; seven crewmen had died at take-off because components of the propulsion system had been replaced at the last minute without sufficient testing. Imprudence and ambition, never the jolliest of bedfellows, were the Leviacrum's overriding legacy. The

Council was so bent on its own pre-eminence, nothing and no one could ever be permitted to steal its thunder.

Yes, they gambled, often at great cost. He shuddered as the mist's unseasonal tinge, something akin to freshly cut grass, pervaded his nostrils.

Steal their thunder? Thunder... If he was right, he and any other survivors here were orphans of the storm—a temporal storm—cast away into the mist of time. He knew he should be furious, but as yet there was nothing on which to vent his fury, no villain, no certain origin of this disaster. For now, the poor lad in his charge was all that mattered.

He spied a group of bedraggled survivors huddled together in the middle of Parliament Street. Two women and about a dozen men. One of the women thumped her fist on her palm and barked like a riled headmistress. She barely seemed to notice him pass and nor was he in the mood to engage a sergeant-major in petticoats.

Bemused middle-aged and elderly gentlemen began filing out of the gentlemen's club, one or two putting their top hats on as though ready for a carefree promenade walk in the bright sunshine. One man with exceptionally large silver sideburns staggered drunkenly off the kerb, but he was not drunk, at least not *only* drunk—blood gushed from his knee. His colleagues carried him back inside. One of them claimed to be a doctor.

At the far end of the road, where London ended half way along Whitehall, a steam-powered car had wrapped around a lamp post. Embrey could see no sign of the driver and he assumed the flash flood had swept him away onto the grassland to the west.

"Is anybody out there? Anybody alive?" he yelled repeatedly to the smashed factories to his right and the quaglike plain to his left. The general dimensions of the phenomenon appeared to be circular—the perimeter curvature had cut through buildings, roads and river alike. It had sliced the back off Big Ben, bisected a Whitehall terrace, and piled a significant volume of Thames water against the interloping escarpment, precipitating the flood. The cool air of storm-battered London would have been sucked beneath this new, warmer air, dragging the airship down with it.

He veered toward a faint reply from high up in the first, least damaged factory. It was a man's voice. But as Embrey waded along a flooded pathway leading behind the terraced buildings of Parliament Street toward the railway track, he frowned. The factory he was making for, if his theory proved correct, would be the central location of the displacement—the phenomenon's epicentre.

A shortish, slightly overweight, middle-aged fellow waving a maroon dinner jacket splashed his way through the flooded foyer entrance. He didn't appear to be hurt. His shock of silver hair resembled an upended, petrified mop and emphasized his thin, square-jawed face and receding hairline.

"What happened out here?" A note of concern, rather than shock, sharpened the man's bass voice. "How big was the radius? Is anyone hurt? Good Lord, the burst was *massive*."

"I'd say roughly a square quarter of a mile," Embrey replied. "Whatever it was, it ripped the heart out of London. Some are dead. I'm on my way to find survivors."

45

"Of course, of course. I'll come with you. A quarter mile—my word! The ionization spread like wildfire. It must have been the storm. Water is conducive to ionised psammeticum—however else could the blast have reached so far but through the raindrops? They were charged *before* the explosion."

Radius? Ionization? Raindrops? "Who are you, sir? What do you know about all this?"

As though the question had defused his mania, the man stopped, his gaze frozen on the little boy. He offered his hand to Embrey. "Cecil Reardon. Unwitting architect of this fiasco, I'm afraid. I'll explain everything later. But first, we must do what we can."

So he's the reckless…

"Lord Garrett Embrey. Considering which way best to murder you, you pompous son of a bitch!" With his free hand, he drew his steam-pistol and thrust it in Reardon's white face. "Do you realize what you've *done*? This is Leviacrum work, isn't it? Those evil—"

"No, old boy. It is most assuredly not." Reardon neither flinched nor batted an eyelid at the eight inches of brass trained on his temple. His calm words unnerved Embrey. "I meant no harm to anyone, and I mean none now. This was all an accident beyond my control."

"Time travel? What madness—"

"Mine and mine alone. And God willing, if my machine has not suffered too much damage, this madness may yet be undone. Embrey—" the lunatic lowered the barrel with his finger, "—this can wait. Let us help the injured."

Clearly mad—he didn't seem fazed by the weapon *or* the cataclysmic events around him—Reardon also had to be the most disarming fellow Embrey had ever met.

Pomp without passion, reserve without fear, manners without guile. It was as though he'd jettisoned all but the most skeletal qualities of what made an English gentleman and then spread his own persona thin over the emptiness inside. The result was distant but oddly endearing. Embrey reckoned that if he didn't owe the man a bullet, he might grow to like Reardon. At the very least, the fellow had kept a cool head, and that was nothing to sneeze at in such a dire situation.

"Come with me." Embrey holstered his pistol and began picking his way through the fallen bricks at the north side of the factory. "And by the way, you managed to bring down an airship," he shot back. "I seriously doubt you can undo *that*."

"Doubt needs no blusher—" Reardon tripped but kept his balance, "—to leave the race red-faced."

Embrey rolled his eyes and fingered his holster. *Don't tempt me, lunatic.*

White steam columned from the ruined eastern portion of Reardon's factory. The area grew hot as they clambered over the collapsed bricks and girders. "This section was a steelworks." Reardon shielded his face from the heat. "It adjoins a larger set-up in the next building. I tell you, the steam cloud—it almost cooked me when the floodwater hit the molten steel. You've never heard a racket like it."

"What exactly do you do, Reardon?" Embrey spied several dark-skinned men busying about the airship's deck. The vessel had to have flown in from Africa.

"I own a few industrial properties in London, one in Liverpool." The man caught up and tossed his dinner jacket around the boy. "There. That'll help keep him dry."

Embrey removed it, handed it back. "The sun will dry him quickest."

White, stencilled letters on the iron airship's bow read *Empress Matilda*. One of the massive twin balloons flew well enough but its sister bobbed low on its rigging, perhaps suffering a slow puncture. The vessel itself lay beached in the mud, a section of the stone embankment having collapsed onto its starboard side, pinning it down. It would not be difficult to free, however. With a little elbow grease and provided the crew could repair and refill the sagging envelope, the airship should be able to fly again.

"If you're thinking what I'm thinking, old boy, then yes, we ought to have ourselves a nice little surveillance bird before long." Reardon retrieved a pipe from his breast pocket and began filling it. "Anything they lack, we will undoubtedly find here in the factories."

"If it ain't all wrecked," the boy argued in a broad Lancashire brogue. Embrey kept a reassuring hand on the youngster's shoulder.

"Sharp lad. You'll go far," the professor said. But that notion made Embrey shiver coldly. Unless they could reverse this awful happening, neither the youngster nor anyone else in fractured London would be going far at all. At least not in society. Perhaps…in lieu of an official criminal sentence, some malign supernatural force had incarcerated Embrey *here* instead, a place so remote that no telegram or ship-in-a-bottle might ever reach another soul.

His face ached from an incessant scowl. He adopted his severest tone. "Reardon, when is this? How far have you flung us, and in which direction?"

"I wish I knew."

"Good God, man. How can we find out?"

"With observation and deduction."

"And you're certain you can undo this thing?"

"Not certain, no, but my machine will have stopped on the last differential sequence. It might not have located 1901, but I have finally found the chronometric settings to enable large scale time travel. My dear Embrey, this is, however heinous the pun, a watershed event for science. Many have died, yes, but consider the import of this misstep. I have conquered time, and without the Leviacrum's meddling. We have done this ourselves, myself and those before me upon whose work I owe a debt. This is—"

"Before you start polishing your laurels, professor, I must remind you that we are *survivors*, not pioneers. These people will not consider themselves privileged—however you spin it—and nor do I. So tread softly, sir. For the love of God, tread softly. If anything should happen to you, we'll be stuck here." Embrey glanced behind him. "And Big Ben will never strike again. You understand?"

"Completely, old boy. I shan't break the news until things have settled."

"See to it."

The African aeronauts lowered a steel ladder for Embrey and his companions to climb on deck. It was a fairly big ship, about a-hundred-and-twenty feet long, with large metal tail fins mounted on each of the four rudder propellers at the stern. A diligent, athletic officer who introduced himself as Tangeni gave the orders. Personnel to and froed between the central, arched-fore-to-aft storehouse and a makeshift hospital area at the bow. Over a dozen men and women in blue British Air

Corps uniforms were being treated for injuries. Among them, unconscious on a generous bed of windproof jackets, lay a striking redhead. She was Caucasian, around twenty-five and wore a midshipman's uniform. Her damp strawberry hair, cropped to little more than a bob, made her look somewhat tomboyish, and the baggy clothes certainly didn't do her figure any favours.

Embrey cocked his head to one side as he gazed at her, and asked Tangeni, "Who is she?"

"Who? *Eembu?* She is captain of the *Empress Matilda*. Everyone on board owes his life to her. She and I, we make promise to eat ice creams on Piccadilly after the storm. That was…before God stepped in."

"Captain, eh?" He'd never have guessed it. *Eembu* more resembled a stowaway cabin girl than a Gannet skipper.

"What are your names, gentlemen?" Tangeni removed his tunic and shirt, revealing a wiry, muscular body bearing many scars. He splashed his face with fresh water from the drinking cask.

"I am Lord Garrett Embrey, this fellow is Cecil Reardon, Professor, and our young friend here—well, I don't believe I heard—"

"Billy Ransdell."

Embrey smiled to himself and ruffled the lad's hair.

"Any of you know what happened?" Tangeni asked.

"As much as you, I'm afraid, old boy." Embrey had always had a strong poker face, and he put it to good use under the African's scrutiny.

Tangeni nodded, threw Billy a wink and then motioned across the deck. "You must stay aboard the *Empress,* of course. From what I see, it is the safest place in London." He tossed one of his crewmen a length of cable. "Until *Eembu* wakes, I am in charge and you are my guests. But she is not badly injured."

"And when she wakes?" Reardon asked.

The acting skipper shrugged.

"We understand." Embrey offered his hand and Tangeni shook it firmly. "Thank you for your hospitality. Where might we find something to eat? I heard Billy's stomach rumble a moment ago."

"On the deck below. Ask for Djimon. Tell him you are friends of Tangeni."

"Much obliged. Oh, and one more thing—" Embrey eyed the intriguing redhead again, "—what does *Eembu* mean?"

The helpful officer smiled, baring his perfect white teeth. "*Eembu* short for *eembulukweya*. In Oshiwambo language it means 'trousers'. Lieutenant Verity Champlain—she get many affectionate nicknames in Africa. But it is unusual for *omukulukadi*—woman—to wear trousers, so that name stayed. It was given to her by a former medicine man now working for the British in Benguela. As he is held in high regard, the name brings her great honour. She is *Eembu,* and she did amazing things today."

"I see. In that case, I can't wait to meet her."

"Nor I," added Reardon.

Embrey escorted Billy to the B-deck hatchway, then glanced back. The reverence these crewmen seemed to have for their female captain was not something he'd encountered before. Striking. Intriguing. And the officer had just referred to her as "amazing"? Just who the deuce *was* she?

Chapter 6

Dislocated

Embrey and the boy looked so snug together in their nest of windproof jackets and blankets in a quiet corner of the fo'c'sle on C-deck, Cecil didn't want to wake them. It had been a long double-day spread across two seasons and two epochs, and dusk was beginning to fall. But he couldn't rest without setting the others' minds at rest. He must at least give the survivors something to hope for.

Then he would figure out when they were, and why the differentiator had failed to locate 1901. Indeed, the latter was the most pressing concern of all, for if he couldn't harness that power, if he was not its master, he might *never* get to find Lisa and Edmond.

He wrapped himself in a cotton blanket and then snatched a few spam ration tins from the supplies Djimon had given them. If the refugees ashore needed more, he would solicit Tangeni for aid right away. He reckoned Embrey might do that if he were awake, and for the time being, Cecil chose to model himself on his young blond comrade—a man of impeccable moral fibre. People needn't see the real Cecil Reardon, the "shadow of a man confined to the rafters of a sad existence," as one ex-colleague had described him in the *Times* last year.

He stole ashore and made his way along the embankment toward Bridge Street. Prolonged, grinding bird caws drew his gaze skyward, but all he saw were the silhouettes of bat-like wings slicing through the gloaming high above. Impossible to classify. In the meantime, he figured the overturned tri-wheeler and its ice cream trailer might make a useful haulage vehicle if the group needed to gather lumber for his furnace or hunt for food.

The survivors had lit a fire on the corner of Parliament Street and Bridge Street, and were roasting meat on makeshift grills.

"I say—dig in, old chap." The nearest gentleman righted a wicker chair on the pavement and patted the seat for Cecil. "You're the lostest thing we've seen for hours. Where the deuce have you been?"

"On the airship over there, with—"

"The darkies, we know. Never been right ones for mixing with civilized folk, our African brothers. Nothing against them, mind you, they're damn good in a scrap, I hear, and they're working wonders over there in Benguela. You know them personally, sir?"

"Not before tonight, but I can vouch for them one and all. They've shown us every kindness."

"Hear! Hear!" an inordinately tall, thin man supping a glass of brandy joined in. "Let's invite our Air Corps friends over. Seeing as we're all stuck here, wherever the devil here is, let us at least start off on the right foot."

"I'll second that," another man bellowed from behind the flames.

"You'd second the plagues of Egypt if you were bloody Pharaoh," shouted another.

"An' goin' off your fizzog, Moses tested a few of 'em on you first."

Laughter roared around the campfire, and Cecil could hardly believe that earlier the same day, London's roots had been ripped up around this very spot. These men, many of them undoubtedly members of the gentlemen's club, seemed to be taking it all in their strides. Or was it merely Dutch courage? He declined a silver hip flask containing what smelled like whisky.

"Do any of you blokes know what happened? The airship crew is understandably bemused. Some fainted with the shock. Have you any ideas?" Cecil tested.

"None of us *blokes* had a rotten clue." The beanpole wiped his nose with a handkerchief. "But the lady here seems to have put two and two together rather ingeniously—says the fellow responsible is probably dead. What was that name again? Rourke? Rankin?"

"Reardon," came a reply through the flames. Cecil recognized Miss Polperro's voice immediately, that schoolmarm abruptness sending a shiver down his spine. Why had it not occurred to him she and her lickspittle cronies would still be in the vicinity? *Ah, hell.* Of course the one person who could blot his copybook *had* to be here waiting with her poisonous agenda. He still had time to sneak away to the ship before she saw his face. Time to regroup, to try another tact. But what excuse could he give? What pressing—

"And your name, sir?" the first man asked innocently.

"My name?" *Um…er…hell.*

"Aye."

54

"Cecil."

"Glad to know you, Cecil." The man loosened his bowtie and shirt collar and then shook hands. "Tomorrow we're heading over to this Reardon's factory, see if we can't put our heads together and figure out what went wrong. Miss Polperro put it nicely. 'Every action has an equal and opposite reaction.' Darned clever."

Cecil scoffed. "I think you'll find that was Newton."

He shrank to nothing as soon as the words tripped from his lips. The woman sprang up and rushed around the fire, probably to confirm her suspicions. Peering over her thick-rimmed spectacles, she gave a sly smirk. "It's Reardon. He tried to trick you all. His name is Cecil all right—Professor Cecil Reardon. *He's* the one responsible for all this."

Another man yelled, "Quick, grab him before he gets away!"

"Whoa! Whoa! I'm not going anywhere. What are you talking about?" He leapt to his feet and backed away from the angry mob, hands out in submission. This could easily turn ugly if he did try to escape. Every instinct tugged at him to flee, but his stubborn brain would not relent. These people needed someone to blame, that was all. After he'd explained himself, they would see reason. "Take your seats and I'll—"

Several furious voices erupted. "String him up!"

"What? *That's insane.*"

"We're not the ones who buggered up time. Let him dangle!"

"You idiots don't know what you're doing!"

"No, leave him be." Miss Polperro's shrill voice barely registered through the cacophony. "We need him to undo what he's done."

Their frenzy would not abate. He kicked and punched at a dozen crazies while they manhandled him off his feet and carried him like a trophy sacrifice to the nearest lamppost. "Hand me that rope—Okay, good and tight—Don't throttle him yet, haul him up first—That's it, round the bastard's neck—Meddle with God's laws? You can argue the toss with him after you swing!—Loop it over, Carswell, that's the way—You three, help me pull on this end—Good one, Delaney, he earned that fist—Now, on three…

"One…two…*three*."

The coarse loop tightened, dug into his windpipe. He could neither gasp nor scream. His fingers couldn't get between the rope and his Adam's apple. A sickening pressure squeezed his tongue from his mouth and his eyeballs up into his brain. His head threatened to explode like an over pumped hydrogen balloon.

Two gunshots rang out.

His feet slapped the pavement and he crumpled in a heap, dazed.

"Back off or we'll see if Whig blood really does run red. That means *you*, Carswell." The voice sounded like Embrey's, but where had he—

A terrible roar unlike anything he'd ever heard flooded Cecil's gasping brain. He coughed, curled himself into a ball on a scrunched tablecloth. Again the roar, this time followed by the dull clap of shoes running in every direction.

"What the hell was that?" someone cried.

"It came from the forest!"

"Everyone get indoors, whatever it is."

Weak hands grappled with his limp shoulder, unable to lift him.

"Ma'am, let me carry him. You'd best get inside." Embrey's voice again. This time, Cecil struggled onto his knees, coughing his guts up. "Easy—I've got you, old boy." The young man's frown made him look a decade older in the firelight. As he crouched, Cecil spied the two pistols steaming in Embrey's hip holsters. "Up you go." The lad heaved him onto his shoulder and made for the gentlemen's club. Another roar sounded much closer this time. Half way up the steps to the front door, Embrey spun northwards, yelled, "Christ Almighty!"

The tip of a long, crooked shadow jerked up the street after them. The ground shook in its wake, and a rampant, thumping rhythm made him fear the building itself would collapse. Embrey halted in the vestibule, lowered Cecil against a glass display cabinet that held bound books, trophies and assorted political guff.

"Here, take this." His young friend offered him one of the steam-pistols. "If anyone makes a try for you, put his seat up for re-election on the spot. Don't hesitate." He spun to the doorway and murmured, "Jesus! I'll be a son of a..."

"W-what is that thing?"

"Beats me, Professor. Something gigantic." Embrey puffed, then touched the flat of the brass barrel to his temple. He moved his lips as though miming a prayer.

Cecil started forward, then crabbed back in horror as a huge lizard-like tail swung over the road outside, knocking the chairs and fire stack over. Sparks and cinders spilled onto the junction. A blood-curdling roar shattered the stained glass window in the reception area to their right. The beast reacted. *Thump, thump.* A monstrous snout poked against the gap, its nostrils as big as rugby balls. Cecil squeezed the moist pistol grip until his fingertips squeaked on the rubber. He daren't move or make another sound. The creature's breaths sounded like the rasps of a slow-moving steam train.

A distant clatter drew it back across the street. The monster reacted to the thunder of falling rubble with another roar. Manmade noise—had that intrigued it? Embrey's pistol shots? What exactly *was* this thing? For the sake of his experiment, he must know.

Embrey tried to hold him back from the doorway but Cecil gained a clear, unforgettable view of the first dinosaur any human had ever seen alive.

"My God, it's colossal."

"And bent on feeding by the looks of it. Down, Professor. Keep down."

Cecil whispered excited mental notes between coughs, while the beast attacked a buckled lamppost in front of a terraced building in which quite a few people—too many people—had gathered. "Four-legged, walks on its rear two, forelimbs longer and more powerful than usual for a *dinosaur.*" He sputtered and couldn't quite believe he'd used that word in a bona fide naturalist endeavour. "Long, low, crocodilian snout, narrow jaws filled with serrated teeth, large, hooked claw on the thumb of each hand, over a foot long. You getting any of this, Embrey?"

"In the seat of my britches, maybe."

"Skull set at an acute angle, not at ninety degrees like most dinosaur skeletons I've seen. I'd say it's close to forty feet from snout to tail. Would you agree?"

"Forty or four hundred, it's got a taste for Londoners. *Look*, it's got someone."

A sickening crunch curtailed the poor bastard's scream as the monster plucked him in its jaw from the second floor of the terraced house opposite.

"And there's nothing we can do," Embrey spat, baring his teeth.

"No, not with steam-pistols."

"We daren't fire a shot. That thing'd bring the roof down on us. Think, damn it, think! Some kind of diversion—lure the bugger away."

He had to hand it to the youngster—Embrey was a natural born leader, graceful under pressure. But there was also that halt-worthy whiff of defiance in his muttering, the noble and self-sacrificing kind beloved of Englishmen over the centuries, feared by their enemies. Personally, Cecil had never experienced it outside of his protection for Lisa and Edmond. For the life of him, he'd never been able to fathom why a man would risk his neck for complete strangers. Nonetheless, he was glad to have such a man at his side.

They watched and waited for the best part of half an hour while the dinosaur stalked up and down Parliament Street probing open windows and doors and exposed sections where the brickwork had collapsed.

"This is no good. It's not giving up. We need the men from the *Empress*." Embrey tugged Cecil's sleeve. "Come, the back of this place is wide open. Let's not dally another minute."

A half dozen members of Parliament cowered in a corner of the smoking room. They watched, speechless, as Embrey and Cecil dashed out over the rubble and across the railway track. What these inebriated swine had done to him a moment ago was so unconscionable, so far outside the realm of possibility, he didn't know whether to pinch himself awake or open fire on the Whigs. For now, he would follow Embrey's resolute lead.

A brigade of African men-at-arms was already piling onto the embankment from the ship. Seeing their rifles made Cecil feel a little safer. Embrey called out, "Where's Tangeni?"

One of the aeronauts pointed back along the embankment. Before he could explain, a terrible roar from the factories forced three of the men to swerve into the mud. A *second* monster burst onto the quayside. It swiped its fore claw at the band of fleeing Africans, felling them like paper dolls. A few stood their ground, opened fire. Embrey's steam-powered shots were gallant but ineffectual at that range. He quickly realised it and desisted, instead helped the men escape toward Cecil's factory, the nearest cover.

"Where's Billy?" Cecil called out.

"With Djimon in—in the fo'c'sle," someone replied, barely hiding his terror.

Embrey held his pistol aloft. "Follow me!" The remaining aeronauts swarmed after him and Cecil as they scampered over the collapsed wire-mesh fence. The dinosaur hadn't finished chewing its latest victim when it lunged into a full sprint. Head low, it stalked them with a bloodlust that reeked of vengeance. It lifted its claws into a taut pianist position under its massive jaws and caught the group within several strides.

At this rate, *none* of them were going to reach the roofed section in time—too much rubble lay in their path, and the monster had its pick of victims.

"Split up," Cecil shouted. "Some of us might make it."

Teeth clenched, Embrey nodded and veered northward, taking eight or nine aeronauts with him while the others quickly overtook Cecil onto the pile of bricks and twisted girders. He glanced behind him and thanked God the beast had stopped to savour its latest meal at the start of the rubble.

A massive claw swung ahead of him and ripped the head off a screaming aeronaut. Cecil ducked, rolled away as the first dinosaur joined the hunt from the south. The combined roars of two leviathans assaulted his eardrums, blanked his mind to anything but imminent, horrific death. In the corner of his eye he glimpsed the silent cogwheels waiting like gloomy cobwebs either side of his miraculous brass machine. It had worked. He'd achieved that much, if nothing more. Edmond would forgive him, Lisa would be proud. Dying screams drowned the clacks of tumbling bricks. He closed his eyes and tucked the pistol muzzle up against his jowl. Better he take his own life than being eaten alive. No regrets to speak of…except one…

"Reardon, no!"

A boy's voice boomed through the night, wrenching Cecil back to life as though it was Edmond calling for him to stay his finger on the trigger. Again the voice climbed high, too high. *"Reardon, wait."* The echo told him it had to be young Billy using a megaphone on the ship's deck. He scanned the site of carnage around him and couldn't believe what was happening.

One of the dinosaurs scrabbled on its side against the hill of bricks, a harpoon cable wrapped around its rear leg. Insanely, someone was driving the tri-wheel car along the embankment. The cable was attached to it—it had *dragged* the monster off its feet. Cecil lowered the pistol in his trembling hand and gasped for air. The cable released. As the lizard struggled upright, the car skidded round for another run, revealing its door-less passenger side. Steam spat and columned from its boiler, shrouding the driver. But as the vehicle gathered speed, Cecil's jaw dropped.

The woman from the *Empress,* the redhead, cradled a harpoon launcher between her legs on the passenger seat. The dinosaur lunged. She fired the iron projectile at its torso, struck a glancing blow—enough for the beast to wheel sideways in agony. She lit a series of flares and tossed them at its feet, then at its monstrous partner's. Slowly but surely, frightened by the flames, the leviathans retreated up the embankment. A last volley of gunfire from the *Empress's* deck proved decisive. The beasts lumbered away toward the northern tree line, their steps shaking London less and less until only a slight quiver remained.

He slumped with his head in his hands and felt, truly for the first time, the gravity of his blunder.

Chapter 7

The Heir and the Air Maiden

Every so often during her six years in the British Air Corps stationed in West and Central Africa, Verity had found herself in a predicament of such rank absurdity, no halfpenny comic writer could have fashioned it. She cringed at the memories: airlifting a pregnant rhinoceros from a narrow gorge hours before an artificial lake burst its banks and flooded the region; singing "For He's A Jolly Good Fellow" to Tangeni on his birthday, in the diving bell, while they suited up to retrieve gold bullion from a sunken Norwegian frigate; being maid of honour at Captain Naismith's wedding to an exiled Congolese princess under the first heavy rainfall in eighteen months; fleeing downriver in a canoe, half-naked, from a tribe dressed up as leopards. And those were merely the ones she could remember. But tonight, she had put them all to shame. Tonight she had crossed over into the realm of the impossible.

"*Eembu,* Tangeni is right. English women crazier *by far* than English men." Kibo shook his head. Her engine man, her brave and brilliant automobile driver.

"You were no slouch yourself, Kibo."

He kissed her hand, nodded politely, then walked away chatting with his engine room pals, who had all come ashore to congratulate him. News of the "harpoon chase" had galvanized the camp for the time being. Tipsy Whitehall gentlemen conversed with salty, dark-skinned aeronauts perhaps for the first time in their lives, but she knew this fraternising would not last. No two peoples could be more different and she dreaded the inevitable hierarchy that would emerge.

Suffering the after-effects of her bump on the head, Verity gave in to her weak knees and climbed back into the car. She sank into the passenger seat, ready to sleep for another day. And next time, the nightmare had better not seem quite so vivid as this one!

No use. The back of her head throbbed, and barbed wire pressed behind her eyes whenever she closed them. Instead, she retrieved the telescope from Tangeni's top coat he'd lent her, and scanned the survivors. Three definite groups appeared to have formed on the embankment. The first pow-wow, in front of the collapsed station house, comprised a strict-looking woman and about fifteen well-dressed gentlemen, all conversing soberly and exchanging compliant nods. They might be trouble if left unchecked. Those lordly types rarely passed up a chance to seize power from any situation.

The second group, not far from the car, consisted of garrulous white gentlemen and black crewmen, plus Reba and Philomena, her two statuesque female riggers, who drew considerable attention from the younger English dandies. Verity raised a smile. No matter what kind of leadership prevailed within the camp, she would do her utmost to encourage both sides to congeal in this manner. On the whole, the Gannet crews she'd served with had proven Anglo-African compatibility beyond doubt. They had pulled together in times of crisis all across Africa. To survive here, in this prehistoric world, that same commitment would be vital.

She turned her gaze to the final group that sat apart on a flat iron door amid the rubble. The small boy she'd met briefly earlier. Kibo had freed his father's body before righting the tri-wheel car with the help of the crew. The poor lad was an orphan, then—and gap-toothed, cute as a button. But who were these other two men he'd grown close to? The older one resembled a cross between a dotty librarian and Captain Nemo, his maroon dinner jacket and shock of silver hair remarkably eccentric.

The younger man bent sideways into the shadows, fiddling with something mechanical in his lap. She couldn't see his face, so she twisted the knob on her spyglass to enlarge the object in his hands. *Hmm, some kind of steam weapon?* She raised an eyebrow when she saw how youthful and handsome he was. He possessed a sleek, distinguished quality that reminded her of a jaguar surveying the jungle from its untouchable bough. It gave him poise and grace and, even at a distance, a striking authoritative air beyond his years. She pegged him as being in his mid-twenties, a similar age to her?

"Um, Tangeni?"

"*Eembu?*" He was only a few feet away, whispering with Djimon.

"Who's the Adonis?"

"Who?"

"The blond man sitting with the boy."

"His name is Embrey." Tangeni paused, perhaps gauging her reaction. "He reminds me of younger Captain Naismith."

65

"How so?"

"He has that same way with him, proud and full of—what's the word—*omafimbo odula.*"

"Seasons?"

"Yes."

She lowered her telescope and blinked at her lieutenant. "You mean he's mercurial? Or steadfast?"

"Yes."

Verity laughed. "My dear old *kaume,* which one is it*?*"

"He is more than meets the eye. And he will not bend from his duty. Other men follow man like that."

"Hmm. Interesting." Tangeni was not wont to voice his admiration for other men freely, and something about the name—Embrey—seemed familiar. She swivelled, slid out of the car and, after composing herself, made her way over for a proper introduction. It might be forward of her but, given the situation, there wasn't time for anything else.

"How are you, Billy? Ready for some supper?" she asked.

The boy flinched and shied away from her, clinging to the young man's tail coat. The latter rose courteously to his feet, took off his coat and draped it around the lad. "It's all right, chief, she's a friend—an aeronaut officer. I'm Lord Garrett Embrey. Enchanted." He offered to take her hand but when she obliged, he couldn't decide whether to kiss it or shake it. It had to be the masculine uniform befuddling him—Tangeni had likely already explained the meaning of *eembulukweya.* She cringed while he glanced at her borrowed trousers and muttered something inaudible. *Hell, why the deuce didn't I change first?*

"Lieutenant Verity Champlain, acting captain." She felt it prudent to assert her authority, if only to keep his title in check. "Nice to meet you, Mr. Embrey." But where had she heard that name before? *Lord,* it was on the tip of her tongue, its import weighing heavier the longer she paused. To hide her frustration, she turned to the other man. "How do you do, sir?"

"Professor Cecil Reardon at your service, ma'am." He had no qualms about shaking her hand and despite his balding, odd-looking features, Reardon made a likeable first impression. His peculiar, exaggerated nod and grin suggested he was socially awkward, trying too hard to ingratiate himself, or he was an extravert who didn't give a fig for social reserve. The only scientists she'd met were the Leviacrum dignitaries she'd ferried from London to Benguela, and they had always kept themselves to themselves. Reardon seemed to be a different fish entirely.

"Please join us, Lieutenant." He set his coat down for her on the edge of a dusty but flat stone wall collapsed upon the rubble.

"Very kind. Thank you." Verity immediately glanced at Embrey, whose attentive gaze now appeared to be undressing her baggy midshipman's uniform. But was it disdain scrutinizing her, or curiosity? Either way, it made her feel uncomfortable. His sharp, sleek face softened into a smile, just for her—even in the dim light from the communal fire on the embankment, his blue-grey eyes were vivid. She swallowed, then pressed her knees tightly together and clasped her hands defiantly on her lap. This was no time for compromising her authority. He was disarming, yes, but Tangeni could still be wrong about him.

"You're the talk of the town—what's left of it." Reardon tapped her knee. "One minute you're warding off bad dreams in a coma, the next you're warding off *dinosaurs*. You'd scarcely credit it, not even if—"

"Bury…" Billy interrupted aloud, checked himself, and then mumbled something that sounded like "Bury oryx."

"What's that? You've seen a dead oryx?" Even Verity cringed at her own patronising tone. Her experience of childhood and children had been abruptly curtailed by her father's posting to the Naval fleet off the coast of Van Diemen's Land. He had subsequently stayed on there as Navy harbour master, a decent job, but Verity's mother had always worried about the effect of transplanting their daughters to such a remote environment with so few children of their own age to play with. Verity had been eight at the time of the move, Bernie eleven. Neither of them had ever had children of their own.

Billy retreated back into his shell and no amount of cajoling from Reardon could tempt him out again.

"Oryx, eh?" Embrey raised an eyebrow. "I fancy our strawberry-haired heroine here will know more about those than us, coming from Africa and all." He gave her a wink and she twitched a polite smile. "So tell us, Lieutenant Champlain—" he began fiddling with his brass weapons again, "—what is your appraisal of the situation? From a military standpoint, how would you go about organising this rabble?"

His tone was playful, his accent mannered to a fault, yet she sensed a note of hostility, especially when he clicked his acid-water cylinder to the chamber of his pistol with a palm-slap, and eyed her sharply.

68

"We need to find out where we are...sooner rather than later," she replied. "In a day or two, if my crew can make the *Empress* airworthy, I plan to take her up for a lengthy reconnaissance. I don't know how we wound up here, or if we can ever return, but *by God* we're going to find out. Last night's fireworks started in this vicinity, in this very factory I believe. Whosoever experimentation is to blame, whosoever insanity smashed us through time, that person is going to have to make himself known—*if* he or she is still alive."

Verity swallowed bitterly, wiped her clammy brow with the sleeve of her tunic. The immediacy of the dinosaur attack had not given her chance to consider anything beyond surviving tonight. And neither had her deep sea diving ordeal really sunk in. She nursed the acute throbbing at the back of her head. She was too tired, too beset by impossibilities to think any more tonight.

"If you'll excuse me, my headache is...I find myself overcome." She got to her feet and, without engaging any of them, stole away to her B-deck cabin fighting a tight, irrepressible ache in her heart. The urge to sob rose and rose like a vinegary high tide until she sank into her pillow and let hot breaths smother her thoughts.

But she didn't cry.

"Oi, Garrett, where's everyone goin'?" Little Billy Ransdell finished nibbling on his chunk of cheese and snatched up his book instead, protecting it from the exodus. The crewmen muttered to one another in their own tongue as they poured out of the low-ceilinged fo'c'sle.

"Djimon says they're holding a big meeting on deck." Embrey, rested and lucid after a sound night's sleep, didn't want to miss the start of this crucial confab. Lieutenant Champlain had apparently invited everyone to attend—an ideal opportunity to hammer out the specifics of surviving as a group in this hostile world. Frankly, he didn't know what to make of her as a woman. Her masculine attire and not-exactly-maternal attempt to engage the boy last night had been a little cringe worthy, but as an officer she had displayed bravery, and she certainly had the respect of her crew. A natural candidate for leadership of the camp. But the notion of anyone having autonomy over him, after what his family had suffered at the hands of British "justice", stuck in his craw as he and Billy clambered up two flights of steps to A-deck.

"Good morning, Embrey." Reardon still hadn't run a comb through his silver mop of hair, but at least it wasn't a stuck-up brush anymore. He was standing on his own against the port bulwark, as far from the other civilian contingent as possible, one hand twitching nervously over the steam-pistol Embrey had given him for protection.

"You slept well?" asked Embrey.

"Quite. I gave a great deal of thought to our situation, though, and to our wayward journey through time. I will explain later when we are alone. Billy, my lad—" he turned to the boy, "—how would you like to help me in the workshop later? I'd love to show you my machine—it's the only one of its kind in the world."

"Ain't it dangerous?" The youngster peered at the ruins of London-that-was.

"Not in the least. I'll explain how it works, and you can—"

The ship's whistle sounded thrice, drawing everyone's attention to the rear of the quarterdeck. The thirty or so African aeronauts immediately formed two fore-to-aft parallel lines at the foot of the stairs leading up to the poop deck. Embrey sighed and leaned back on the bulwark beside Reardon. This ceremony might be standard practice on a Gannet ship, but he fancied it was more for the civilians present, a display of discipline to assert a captain's right of overall command.

How would this gaggle of male politicians react to a woman calling the shots? And she was only a youngish lieutenant at that. No, it would be far better for diplomacy's sake if one of them took up the mantle or, better still, someone as proficient in upper social circles as he was with a rifle.

Why not himself, the son of a marquess?

The two columns stiffened at the sound of boot steps approaching from the captain's cabin beneath the stairs. Heads cocked and tongues wagged throughout the civilian contingent gathered on the starboard side. Embrey merely rolled his eyes. Anyone would think a maharani had arrived on deck.

"As you were." Her officious, slightly accented voice relaxed the ranks and she began climbing the iron staircase.

Sunlight speared between the fidgeting balloons overhead, reflecting dazzlingly off the upper rain-minted steps. The starboard aft stay cable groaned as it compensated for the left envelope bobbing in the web of harness lines above. It was a crisp morning, cucumberish to the taste, and the pungent saline breeze

71

reminded him strongly of Devonshire. The sun faded, giving him a clear view of Lieutenant Champlain.

"Good God." Embrey almost choked on his own utterance. He loosened his shirt collar, cleared his throat, for the officer about to address the ship's company bore almost no resemblance to the tomboy aeronaut from yesterday. Her khaki pith helmet sat neatly on a blaze of cropped red hair, emphasizing her elfin features and small-but-sticky-out ears. She looked around twenty-five. The years of African sun had kissed her skin to a tender cream-and-pink complexion, similar to that of his uncle, who had never tanned despite long periods of exposure. Her white shirt-waist blouse had puff top sleeves and soft, vertical lace on an ample bosom. Embrey's eyes widened at her flared, corduroy jodhpurs and leather half chaps over paddock boots. The ensemble was so bold for a woman in the Air Corps, so utterly her own, it struck him dumb.

So *this* was why the crew revered her. "Unique" did not do her justice. The only things missing were her riding crop and hunting rifle, and she likely had those in her cabin. Instead, Tangeni merely handed her a tan bush jacket, which she considered putting on but rather plonked onto the steps behind her.

"Ladies and gentlemen, thank you for your show of solidarity." She cleared her throat. "I will make this as brief as I can, as we have a lot of work to do. Time travel is an alien concept to me, and I don't presume to understand how we got here or how we might return. For my part, this is a challenging survival situation, nothing more, nothing less. I am First Lieutenant Verity Champlain of the British Air Corps' Fifth Gannet Squadron, and acting captain of the *Empress Matilda*. This fine gentleman—" she motioned below her, "—is my second in command, Lieutenant Tangeni. Between us, we shall try to provide protection for everyone here, and also to offer this ship as a safehouse whenever we are threatened. At other times, I must insist only my crew and a select few guests be permitted residence here. Unless we can find a source of fresh water nearby, we will need to fly the *Empress* regularly to collect it, and also to explore. Given last night's attack, it is prudent to insist no one venture near the forest on foot unless with an armed party."

She removed her helmet to massage the back of her head and glimpsed Embrey out of the corner of her eye. His pulse quickened. He offered her a friendly nod.

"As I was saying—" She paused, glanced at him again but this time, to his amusement, she bunched her face up into a flustered, irritable frown. She put the helmet back on. "We shall endeavour to provide protection and that includes from troublemakers within the group. My crew is not here to police your streets but I can assure you no crime will be tolerated. My one inviolate rule either on or off the ship is that no one, and I mean *no one*," she addressed the gaggle sharply, "is to hinder Professor Reardon's work in any way. As I understand it, he is our guarantor for a return to our own time. If any of you so much as lay a finger on him, that person will face summary punishment. And if there is even a whiff of another lynching party, I will not hesitate to execute every last member. Do not cross me on this."

She glared into the wave of dissenting chatter on the starboard side until it dissipated. "Now, on a more positive note," she said, "I think it is time you choose a leader from among you. The coming days or weeks, or however long it takes Professor Reardon to reconfigure his machine, are going to require careful planning and coordination. I will confine my office to this ship and to the repulsion of outside threats. I will not interfere in your governing of this…London. But may I suggest you select a leader here and now, so the matter can be put to rest? Is that acceptable?"

"Hear! Hear!" most of them agreed.

Reardon tugged Embrey's sleeve and whispered, "Go on, old boy. Put yourself forward."

Pride flushed through him, shot him up off the bulwark. Embrey knew with every drop of blood coursing through his frame that he had the attributes to lead this group, to become the man his father had always seen in him. This wasn't some shady boardroom— political conspiracies held no sway over a stark survival situation like this. He was a man of action, a survivor, and his voice should be heard. But as he stepped forward, thumbed his lapels to announce his candidacy, the lady captain shouted above the din, "Might I suggest Lord Embrey as a possible name for the ballot?"

He bowed, more surprised than ever, and Lt. Champlain produced for him the warmest smile he'd seen her give yet. But why had she recommended him like that? They'd barely met last—

"Emphatically not," a furious voice piped up from across the deck. "Embrey? The son of a traitor—the Beast of Benguela? I'd as soon vote for that monstrosity that attacked us last night. Of all the nerve! Marquess Embrey rots in hell, I hope!"

"Who said that? Let him step forward. Blasted coward!" Embrey drew his pistol and snatched the other from Reardon's belt. He barged through the lines of crewman and, hissing expletives, stalked the fleeing gaggle, ready to wreck the first man who confronted him. "Yellow bastard! Where are you? I challenge any man here and now—either qualify that accusation in a fair duel or I will kill the next offender in cold blood. I swear to God, the next man who impugns my family name eats a bullet!"

Over two dozen terrified gazes could not sate his hatred. These were the scum who'd sat idly by while two innocent men had been scapegoated and hung—two well-respected men of impeccable quality. His uncle, his *father*. How dare the vultures crow about it. Fury boiled and would not subside, not even when Tangeni and Kibo carefully escorted him back to his place at the bulwark, where he received an understanding hand on the shoulder from Reardon.

"I vote for Miss Agnes Polperro," a resolute male voice announced. "She is a delegate from the Leviacrum Council, not to mention one of the brightest ladies I've met. We are lucky to have her, and it would give equilibrium to the leadership. One lady to run the *Empress,* another to run London."

"Seconded," a gruff man added.

"Aye!—Hear! Hear!—Capital idea!—Three cheers for Miss Polperro!—Hip, hip, hooray! Hip, hip, hooray…"

During the final cheer, Reardon leaned over and spoke into Embrey's ear, "That's us confined to the ship, old boy. Miss Polperro incited the lynching last night, and she'll have the knife in you for sure. This is a black mark on the whole show."

"We'll see." Embrey handed him back one of the pistols.

He looked up to Lt. Champlain, hoping for a friendly acknowledgement, a gesture of reassurance that she bore him no ill-will despite the altercation and despite the fact she'd been publicly humiliated alongside him. She had, after all, vouched for the son of a convicted traitor.

Her icy gaze chilled him to the core. He stormed away and, against the boy's protests, left the ship at once, hatred for the world and all its epochs broiling inside him. High over the collapsed station house, the face of Big Ben read five past eight.

It would read five past eight the next time he had to kill someone.

Chapter 8

The First Reconnaissance

The Rt. Hon. Reginald Kincaid, Assistant Secretary of the Treasury, and at eighty-one the eldest member of the group, finished his eloquent eulogy on the damp lawn of Speaker's Green. The thirty-four graves were neat and egalitarian, no concessions made for race, class or gender. It was unanimously agreed that this was the most apropos resting place for those fallen—in London soil, not in the alien dirt of prehistory.

Tangeni handed Verity the fourteen cotton badges they'd cut from the dead aeronauts' uniforms. Each had the BAC insignia sewn onto it. With a heavy heart, she nailed them to the wooden ground pegs at the head of each grave, remembering the scores of African friends she'd lost in the corps over the years. Visualizing their faces was difficult—the recollection was broader, more enveloping, the kind of bittersweet cloak that wrapped the word "family." Over the past several years, she'd bonded to these brave men and women as permanently as any friends she'd made in England or in Van Diemen's Land.

When she finished, Tangeni laid a comforting hand on her shoulder. Kibo saluted the graves, tears streaming down his proud face, while Reba and Philomena each blew a kiss to their fallen comrades. Reaching London was supposed to have been a homecoming or a chance at a new, better life for the *Empress's* crew—most of whom had never seen England before. But where was this if not London? Verity felt as though she had one foot on home soil and another in a nightmare version of it. Any second now, one reality or the other would come crashing down. But right now, she was captain of purgatory and nothing seemed to belong, including herself.

"They get to stay in London. Their troubles are over now." Tangeni dabbed his eyes with his handkerchief. "But we, *Eembu*…we are no closer to Piccadilly than Angola. And no ice cream in sight either."

Miss Polperro glared at him as though he'd just blasphemed. Her thick-rimmed spectacles intensified her cold, grey eyes, but Verity didn't know what to make of her. The men of Whitehall had vouched for her. She had a position of some note in the Leviacrum hierarchy. But what would she be like in a practical situation that demanded survival, not bureaucracy? Time alone would tell.

"No, no ice cream yet, my friend," Verity replied. "And you're right, Piccadilly has seen better—"

She felt a tug on the waist of her blouse and looked down. "Boy? What's the matter?"

Billy didn't reply, instead tugged even harder as though he wanted her to follow him. Then he yanked Tangeni's tunic, as well.

"Sorry about this." Embrey interceded, trying his best to calm the boy without using force. "He's had a rough time. Rougher than any of us." But the lad cried and wouldn't stop pulling, and Embrey's fake smile began to fail him. Colour filled his cheeks. Verity didn't know where to look. This marvellous-looking man was inches away and turning beetroot, and she was honour-bound to despise him? No, she *did* despise him. His father and uncle had colluded with the enemy, facilitated the assault on the Benguela Leviacrum—the fire that had killed Bernie. *Her* Bernie.

"Stop it, Billy." Embrey shook the boy's shoulders. "I said *stop it.*"

The lad sobbed even louder and wouldn't stop pulling. Embrey's resulting scowl appeared so cruel and uncalled for, Verity suddenly hated him like she'd never hated anyone since the day Father's telegram had arrived…with news of Bernie…

She slapped Embrey's face with all her might. The crack drew everyone's attention. Stunned, he let go of the boy and withdrew, stumbling in the mud as he turned. The hushed voices and Kibo's tearful frown and the lad's incessant sobbing and the realisation that she'd hit a man at his most vulnerable strained her heart's defences.

Bitterness welled up. The weight of the surge was greater than she could handle but spying the *Empress* steeled her resolve. A captain should never cry in front of her crew. She needed somewhere to hide, yet the entire camp was watching. Her bottom lip quivered, so she wiped her mouth with her sleeve.

Tangeni appeared to glimpse her emotion as he said, "*Eembu,* I think Billy has something to show us." He took the youngster's hand and then motioned for her to do likewise. "Lead the way, young master."

Like rummaging through an old drawer, being led by a child through the detritus of London drew long-forgotten memories. The way she'd once seen the world—not aggregated and mastered but magical. A child's mind could not grasp Whitehall and Westminster. They were too imperious, too cold. They were permanent things the world could not do without, like soil and sunshine. So what could a child possibly make of those things in ruins?

Bernie had loved the empire, and Verity had grown to love it. She sighed. When Bernie had died, that empire she'd revered, put her life on the line for, had collapsed for Verity the way London had just collapsed for Billy. She now saw it clearly for the first time, without the corps' camaraderie to buoy her patriotism. She was living in the shadow of that day, and all this—flying Gannets, fighting wars, cropping her hair—was in Bernie's name. Strangely, it all seemed to fit but why hadn't she admitted it before now? Had no part of *Verity* wanted to join the Air Corps? If not, why was she such a talented aeronaut? Why had she loved her time in Africa? Loved her time in the air, on the waves, under the waves...?

"This was your father's wagon?" Tangeni asked Billy as they reached the uncoupled rear section of the tri-wheel vehicle. It was square, white, and was mounted on two wheels. Two painted red bands bisected all sides.

"What have you got in here, Billy?" Verity asked.

The lad unbolted a well-concealed door in the rear panel, opened it and climbed inside. He quickly returned with a metal container the size of a shoebox and two spoons. Without making eye contact with her or Tangeni, he prised the lid off with a spoon handle and passed the open container to Verity. "You said there were no ice cream," he said in his thick Lancashire accent. "'Ere you go. That there's me favourite—raspberry an' vanilla. It'll be soft by now but taste'll still be there."

Tangeni looked at her, grinned with astonishment, and then dipped his finger in the ice cream. "*Omashini…ojuice.* It is wonderful." He thanked Billy for the spoon and delved into the half-full trough. Verity joined in.

"Mm, that's divine," she said. "And you're full of surprises, my young friend." She kissed Billy's forehead. He looked up at her for the first time, a beatific smile lighting his pale face. Tangeni wiped the lines of tears from the lad's cheeks with his handkerchief. As soon as the youngster saw the warmth in Tangeni's eyes, he climbed back into the vehicle. Moments later, he returned with a spoon for himself.

"Reba, is that stay line doubled in?"

"Yes, *Eembu.*" The rigger wiped her brow while the sun blazed relentlessly.

Verity took a swig from the captain's hipflask she'd filled with the lemonade Billy had given her. The lad had doled out the best of his father's refrigerated supplies to herself, Tangeni, Reardon, and that son of a bitch, Embrey, whom Billy followed everywhere. Apart from a few bottles of sarsaparilla and flavoured water, the remainder of the ice cream wagon's supplies were either wafer cornets or melted desserts. She'd given those to the Whitehall group, whose meagre rations, for the time being, would have to be shared from the contents of four residential kitchens, the larder and wine cellar in the gentleman's club, a few freight crates containing foodstuff salvaged from the collapsed station house, and one cold dinner for twelve impeccably laid out moments before the disaster had hit. Not much to feed over two dozen mouths over an indeterminate period of time. No, as soon as the *Empress* returned, they would have to organise hunting and perhaps fishing parties to procure a sufficient diet.

"Tangeni—peacock—are those ballonets filled and secured?" Her second in command had been strutting about the quarterdeck admiring his new first lieutenant's insignia ever since he'd finished the steam-methane reforming operation, his specialty, over an hour ago.

"Aye, Captain. Endothermic reaction successful, the pumps and pipes held, the ballonets have new life."

She whispered, "What do you make of that bastard Embrey roaming about the ship, free as you like? Seditious scum like that, he's campaigned against the admiralty ever since his father and uncle were hanged. I wouldn't bet against him being in cahoots with the enemy all along. Damned traitor—he should be clapped in irons."

"Sorry, *Eembu,* what was the question?"

She rolled her sleeves up irritably. "No question. Just miffed at the thought of him having free access like this. Look at him, hand behind his back, hobnobbing with the crew like some condescending VIP. Damn him."

"Would you rather he be left to the politicians? They've already shown their idea of diplomacy, no? I wouldn't bet against his neck being stretched by Miss Polperro and those old sharks with sideburns."

"Don't be impertinent. The boy wants him here, so he stays. But I've got my eye on him. Mark my words, if he so much as belches a seditious—"

"All repairs to the cables and envelopes completed, Captain." Tangeni clearly wanted to change the subject. She let it slide this time. No one else had heard, and from his combative demeanour she inferred Tangeni still held Embrey in higher regard than she did. Maybe she *was* treating the young marquess unfairly. Maybe he was made of truer stuff than his antecedents. But her family honour and her allegiance to the crown demanded she keep him at arm's length. His very name forfeited his right to be presumed innocent. By dint of association, he was a traitor.

"Very well, unhook anchor stays and clear away," she said. "Three-quarter engines, four points to port. Then steady on my mark."

"Aye."

As Tangeni relayed her commands, she ignored a solicitous stare from one of the gentlemen passengers, a young buck with a bandage over his brow who had politely offered his expertise in geology and botany to the expedition. Mr. Briory hadn't been able to keep his eyes off her. He was dark-haired and a little overweight—the opposite of Embrey and therefore a safe choice—and she didn't find him particularly attractive. He was guileless and sweet, though. She might have liked him before she'd joined the corps.

The *Empress Matilda* rose smoothly away from the derelict site, her ballonets taut and well-balanced. The propellers hummed at the stern, and white steam clouds billowed out of the port and starboard exhaust vents. Verity's breath caught. The gorge behind Big Ben widened considerably a half mile westward—they had escaped a deadly abyss by an infinitesimal fraction in the vastness of time and space. In that regard, they had been fortunate. In many others, however—

"Captain! Water!" Reba hollered down from the bough nest—her basket affixed to the centre of the two lower cables joining the balloons. "Water off the port bow!" She mimed the breaststroke, indicating it looked deep and big enough to be either a sea or a large lake.

A hopeful glow lit Verity's heart. She ran to the port bulwark and looked through her telescope. The gap in the forest stretched on past the escarpment for about a mile, forming a grassy bottleneck before it met a sudden decline, possibly a short cliff. The beach beyond appeared to be full of rocks and kelp. An impenetrable sea mist masked her view of the west past the tree line. To the east, a procession of large, lumbering creatures dominated the beach as the coastline curved northeast toward a region of flat, low-lying sediment. Three or four geysers spewed their hot vapour over the flatland, giving the region a torrid, inhospitable appearance.

"Reardon, where are you? Reardon?" She waited for him to bluster aft with little Billy in tow. "Oblige me with your observations. This is as much your reconnaissance as ours."

"On my way, Ver—Captain."

"And you too, Mr. Briory." He was standing at her shoulder in an instant, a mite too close for comfort. She stepped away. "Can you pinpoint this prehistoric age, sir?"

"I would say somewhere in the mid-Cretaceous." He beat Reardon to the punch. The professor had already opened his mouth ready to speak but now closed it with chagrin. His curt nod to the younger man amused Verity. The idea of two scholars duking it out over the science of their prehistoric prison—where else would she get to hear *this* conversation?

"Do you concur, Professor Reardon?" she egged him on.

"Hmm, perhaps a trifle earlier, I'd say." Stroking the stubble on his chin, he gazed eastward toward the geysers. "That alluvial plain is in its infancy, and this whole region—likely covering northern France and southern England—appears to still be in its submerged state. The land has yet to tilt, and the great Wealdon Lake has barely begun to empty."

Briory shook his head and gave a smirk. "I beg to differ, sir. You're right about the alluvial plain but we have seen so little of the region, how can we possibly say how much is flooded and how deep the water is?" He lifted his head superciliously, then leaned out over the bulwark and roved his index finger over the forest below. "The plants give a clearer indication. Look at the trees. We have oak and maple, and in the south and east I noticed only a few Jurassic ferns. The angiosperms have taken hold, and the more primitive gymnosperms are struggling. Note the emergence of colour on the edges of the forest—those are early flowering plants, pollinated by the first bees, but they are widespread enough to indicate the evolution has been in action for some time. I believe we are in the mid-Cretaceous, about ninety million years ago. There are—"

"Bury oryx…onyx."

"Don't interrupt," Briory scolded young Billy.

"Oh, pipe down, you unctuous little organ grinder." Reardon glared at Briory. Then with a defiant glint in his eye, he lifted the boy onto his shoulders. "What was that about an oryx?" he asked gently.

85

"Yes, it's the second time you've mentioned that," Verity said.

Billy lifted his pullover and retrieved a thin, cloth-bound book he'd tucked into his trousers. "It's in 'ere. I don't know 'ow to say it proper." He opened it at the sketch of a large dinosaur, *exactly* like the one they'd encountered on the first night. "That bloody big 'un nearly got you, Cecil," he went on. "I ain't much good at readin' but I knew it from t' picture. That's it there. Bury… Barry…"

Verity leaned over to help him. "Baryonyx! That's *it*. Well done, Billy." Touching his shoulder, she read on, "A piscivorous predator from the early Cretaceous." The three of them glanced over at Briory, who pouted and walked off with an *hmmpf*. She'd have loved to hear Reardon's mumbled words of victory, but Billy tapped the page, eager for her to continue. She scanned the text for facts they didn't already know about the monster, while promising herself she'd study the whole book later. "Piscivorous means 'fish-eater'…the baryonyx swipes at fish with its powerful claw…like a grizzly bear. It lays four to six eggs. Scientists think it might—"

"Forget the homework." Reardon leaned over the side, thrust his arm out. "There they are! On the shore—big as life."

A wasps' nest stirred in Embrey's stomach. These extraordinary animals were bigger than anything above the waves in the twentieth century, and they were also deadlier. If they attacked London again, or this airship whilst it was in dock, the loss of life could be catastrophic. The beach lay a little over a mile from the camp. If dinosaurs were at all territorial—he'd encountered firsthand the violent reactions of South American predators against interlopers in their marked territory— these monsters *would* return to London sooner or later.

They lumbered back and forth across the black and grey beach, taking turns to eat from a rhinoceros-sized carcass while the other guarded the meal. Neither paid any mind to the *Empress*. At five hundred feet up, the airship would be like just another cloud.

Tangeni approached from the bow. "Lord Embrey, have you heard? The professor, he says this is all fresh water. A giant *etale* from ancient times. That is good news, no?"

"Tremendous news! I daresay a big piece of our survival puzzle is solved." He gazed aft along the deck to where Reardon and Billy were busy reading a book with Verity Champlain. The wasps roused again. Being *persona non grata* under *her* command, the tainted strawberry tart, stung his heart. He despised feeling helpless as much as he hated her magnanimity. If his name offended her so much, she needn't have allowed him on board the *Empress* at all. The fact that she had, and that he'd accepted, slighted him more and more as he thought on it. Trapped was not the word—he was in purgatory. No one wanted him here. He was the prehistoric pariah. And Captain Champlain had become the icy figurehead for the empire's unforgiving rule—a rule that had cost him everything.

"God Almighty! Why does she make me so angry?" He clasped his hands behind his head and pressed the palms into his scalp.

"*Eembu* has that way with her." Tangeni's probing stare seemed to pick apart Embrey's agony like clockwork. "She almost make married two years ago, to the young vizier governing Zanzibar—a man of great intelligence—but the Sultan's rebels attacked him days before the wedding. When she learned of the plot, *Eembu* swam to his island home to warn him but she was too late. He died in her arms, poisoned, and the assassins, they were caught by the British Navy. That night, *Eembu* sneaked aboard the ship and slit their throats one by one, then threw their bodies to the sharks. For this she receive three-month suspension from the admiralty." Tangeni swallowed a lump in his throat. "Of all the men and women I've served with, no one faces *oshipongo*—danger—like she. Lieutenant Champlain has no compromise. That is why she makes you angry."

"I see." Embrey glanced again at the ginger-haired captain, who was now laughing with Reardon and young Billy. For a few warm moments, all ill-will evaporated from the airship, and he felt like walking over to her and straightening this whole thing out. Any animus between them had been created by proxy, by pride. They could easily cast it aside if they wished.

A chill gust raked the deck, snapped him back to his senses. He watched the two dinosaurs squabble needlessly over their prize on the beach.

"I'm afraid my wound runs even deeper." He patted Tangeni's shoulder. "My own country has turned against me, brother—it won't rest until it has extinguished my family name altogether."

"I have heard. A terrible thing, to be hated by one's own tribe. But Professor Reardon believes in you, and so does young Billy. As for *Eembu*, she wears her sister's memory like war paint—it reminds her that she lives for two, and also fights for two. You are the closest she has come to finding, what is the word? Avenging?"

"Vengeance?"

"Yes. She will treat you as an enemy until you can convince her to believe in you."

Embrey scrubbed his face with his hands. "I may need some help there, brother. But I tell you what, you can let Lieutenant Champlain know that I'm willing to forgive the unprovoked blow she struck, on one condition—"

"And that is?"

He swung round and almost swiped her with his elbow.

Luckily, she ducked. "Of all the clumsy, skull-faced…"

Maybe not so lucky.

"My apologies," he stuttered.

The woman's pursed lips held venom. "Well?" she snapped. "You were saying? You would deign to forgive my wholly *warranted* affront on one condition?"

"Yes, one condition. That you shuffle up and down the deck on your arse whilst singing 'Burlington Bertie From Bow.'" He stood tall, glared back with interest. "What's wrong? Feel like hitting me again?" Offering his chin felt a tad much, but *Jesus,* she was infuriating.

"How about throwing you over the side, fop?" Several crewmen and the two statuesque women now stood behind her, meaning she couldn't possibly back down.

Neither would he.

"You talk a good game, Red. How does the rest of it go? 'I flap my lips and you drown in spit'? Pathetic.

You're a pantomime king in petticoats—the least you can do is wear them."

"One more word and you'll dangle from the keel. Follow in your father's footsteps...or should I say his last dance."

"*Whore!*"

"Bastard."

He drew both his pistols and thrust them at her heart. "Say that again."

She reached nonchalantly over her shoulder and kept her hand there until a crewman passed her a revolver. Without even breaking her stare, she cocked the hammer with her thumb and pointed the gun at his forehead. "This is getting tiresome. Djimon, Tangeni, lock this traitor in the brig."

"*Eembu?*"

"Don't argue with me. He's not about to shoot. He doesn't have it in him. His sort whispers treason from the shadows, sends others to do his dirty work. The rich only stay rich because they don't get involved in the fighting they start. Look, you can see it in his yellow eyes. Like father, like—"

"*Enough!*" Embrey sidestepped quickly. In one fluid motion he dropped one of his own pistols, dragged her flush against him and disarmed the bitch. Back to the bulwark, he held a pistol barrel to her temple and yelled, "Back off! All of you."

"Do it. But he's bluffing," she advised her crew—correctly. Unbearably. Did *nothing* faze her?

His situation was impossible and he had nowhere to go. Better to live and fight another day than force the crew's hand. *Okay, Garrett, you lose this round.* His pulse hacked at his right shoulder, leaving him breathless. He lowered his sidearm and the bitch eased herself free.

An overhead cable snapped and the airship lurched to port, hurling Verity into him again. Her momentum threw them both over the rail. Embrey tossed his weapon onto the deck and snatched for the bulwark. Too late! His fingers slipped and he plummeted.

Verity's arms wrenched tight around his solar plexus, mashed up against his rib cage. The jolt of her catch punched the breath from his lungs. A million flecks of diamond dust from the waves below blinded him. Somewhere inside the shock, distant bird caws competed with a close, intermittent hiss.

"Swallow it," she demanded into his ear hole. "I can't hold you much longer. My legs…they're wrapped round…the rail. *Embrey, do you hear me?* You need to…climb up me."

The *Empress* lurched again. Verity's grasp slipped to crooked fingertips. They shook with the strain, and Embrey felt as though his invisible lifebelt was ripping loose. The diamond grave called imperceptibly. The soft fabric of her blouse caressed his cheek. It stayed death with a tickle, beckoning him from his daze.

"Verity?" The airship listed badly and seemed to be in freefall. He anchored his arms around her bare waist, then reached up and hoisted himself up by her jodhpurs. "Hold on," he told her, "I'm almost there."

Tangeni and Reardon gripped her half chaps. High above, a formation of five enormous birds scythed between the balloons. Their bites at the canopies rocked the entire ship. They were piercing the ballonets. Embrey heaved himself up into Reardon's grasp, and two more aeronauts arrived to haul him aboard.

"Look out!" a cry came from above—from Philomena perched in the bough nest, fending off the monstrous birds with her grappling pole.

Embrey followed her gaze low to the port bow, where a rogue flier had begun its unstoppable climb for Verity. Its wingspan had to be around forty feet—more like a dragon's than a bird's—but the flapping membrane was translucent and wafer thin.

Pterosaurs!

Several aeronauts emerged from B-deck toting rifles, but the *Empress's* violent shudder spilled them into each other. A familiar *hiss-crack* sounded from somewhere aft. Immediately the pterosaur flinched as a fresh hole appeared in the middle of its right wing. Someone had had the right idea. *My steam-pistol?* He scanned the deck and spotted the second weapon right away. It was teetering on the brink several feet from him, beneath the bulwark. The bird opened its long beak and gave a gutteral caw. *Christ.* Why hadn't Tangeni pulled Verity up yet? She had to be snagged on something.

Embrey dove for the pistol and fired a snapshot. *Hiss-crack!* The bullet clipped the pterosaur's snout but didn't stop it. He could almost drop something onto it at this range. Instead, he took aim and pipped the creature right between its eyes. More shots rang out aft. Some hit. The pterosaur folded its wings, gave a spastic flutter, and then writhed as it fell.

He helped Tangeni and Reardon free the buckle of Verity's half chaps from a twisted rivet she'd ripped loose from the bulwark post. She was lightheaded when they hauled her aboard. Embrey and Tangeni steadied her while she regained her bearings. The blood had rushed to her head. Her face was almost purple.

"Will you be all right?" he shouted above the pterosaur shrieks and volleys of gunfire. "I need to join the fight."

She nodded blankly. Tangeni reassured him. "I'll take it from here. You try and pick them off as they clear the balloons. And get Reardon to take Billy below. This no place for a boy."

Embrey dashed aft to the quarterdeck. Reardon was already escorting young Billy below—one less problem to solve, at least. All around the ship's hindmost section, riflemen ducked in sequence to avoid passing pterosaurs and then leapt up in the same order to unleash a volley. He couldn't speak for their marksmanship, but these African aeronauts were stalwarts. He climbed to the poop deck and took the place of a man who'd bled to death. The three fatal gouges in his chest suggested monstrous talons had gored him. Embrey fired his remaining bullets and then used the dead man's rifle to pick off the last pterosaur. The other three fliers fled eastward above the geyser clouds, regrettably in perfect formation.

As he helped his injured brothers-in-arms down to sick bay—five were wounded, though not seriously—he met Verity's gaze on the quarterdeck. Blouse torn and hanging loose, fiery hair licking the breeze, she looked a fright. Yet, unkempt, she was also insanely beautiful, more unreal and more desirable than ever.

The urge to gush his relief pressed hard against the cork in his heart. Surely they couldn't be enemies after *this*. Their mutual gaze held. An insensible longing to take her in his arms threatened to overpower him. Then he remembered his name.

They exchanged brief nods instead.

Chapter 9

The Captain's Cabin

What was it with everyone vouching for Lord Embrey like he was some kind of Nelson or Wellington? Yes, he had a knack for being in the right place at the right time, and he was handy with a rifle, but in case they'd all forgotten, *she* had saved *his* life over the side of the ship that afternoon.

"Either you admit him or I say precisely nothing on the subject of time travel," Reardon protested, arms folded as he sank back in his chair. Her new cabin barely had enough room to seat two guests, so Tangeni had emptied most of Captain Naismith's belongings and replaced them with three more chairs from the officers' mess.

"And you already know my opinion." Tangeni fingered the lieutenant's insignia on his tunic. "Without Lord Embrey, Professor Reardon would have been hanged and the flying dinosaur would have snatched you for certain." He turned away. The two men sat in complicit silence, watching the oil lamp.

Marvellous. I'm being bullied by my own personal press-gang!

But at this moment, Reardon and Tangeni were the two most important men to her in London. For the sake of the mission, it behoved her to keep them happy. And after all, her boycott of Embrey was personal. If rescinding it would benefit the plight of the camp…so be it.

"Very well, let him in." She glared at her first officer but he merely shrugged in reply. Reardon opened the door, called for Embrey. A cool gust brushed her face and made the lamp flame flicker while the handsome blond traitor strolled in.

"Where's Billy?" Reardon asked his aristocratic comrade.

"Below, eating supper with Kibo and Djimon. The lad's become quite popular since he pipped the pterosaur."

"With your steam-pistol, was it not?" Verity seized the chance to segue into civil conversation with him. Ignoring their rancour altogether seemed the only way to proceed. And he looked improbably dashing in the wavering light.

He addressed her briefly, "Yes, ma'am. My pistol." His glance ricocheted off her. "Reardon, this had better be deuced important. The lads in the fo'c'sle are setting up a game of gin rummy. They fancy they'll own my estate before morning, while I beg to differ—"

"Oh, you needn't play gin rummy to count your good fortune, old chap." Reardon's subtle rebuke made Verity smile.

"I see. And to what do I owe this privilege?"

"We're to confer on…all the essentials of our survival," the professor replied. "Most important, Verity here is eager to know how I plan to return us to our own time."

Embrey looked up, striking electric sparks in her gaze. "The lady has a healthy curiosity."

Yes, and the gentleman *is eyeing my breasts.* She attempted to repel him with a scowl. He continued to watch her, to study her. She cleared her throat, distracting him.

"*Eembu* is thirsty?" Tangeni rose and stood between her and Embrey, perhaps to dispel the awkward moment.

She looked at up at her first officer. "Yes. There's a kettle of hot water on the sideboard."

"I know. I gave it to you."

"Really? Fiddlededee." She shook her head at how girlish that sounded.

"Tea?"

"No. I'll have something with a little bite."

"A posset? I see you have the ingredients already prepared."

"I do?" She deflected Embrey's latest questing glance, and gathered herself. "Yes, of course I do."

"I know. I gave them to you." Tangeni began whistling tunelessly to himself.

Why, the smug...

Embrey called over to the Namibian, "I'll have a brandy, my good man—neat, and you can keep the spoilers."

"I apologize, Lord Embrey. Spoilers?"

Verity sighed and crossed her legs. "He means he just wants the brandy, Tangeni."

"Ah. Sorry, my English is coming on in leaps and bounds but—"

"I know. I gave it to you." Verity flicked him a wink, which tickled him no end.

"I will forego my libation," Reardon interrupted, "if the three of you will desist from this childish parlour game. Good Lord!" His birdlike head pivots, eyeing each of them in turn, reminded Verity more of a flustered headmaster than a scientist whose genius potentially rivalled that of Sir Isaac Newton. "Now, back to the business at hand?"

"Go ahead, old boy. You mustn't let our parlour game perturb you." Embrey threw him a wink. "We're all ears—truly. Look. Tangeni's are whoppers."

Verity cleared her throat. "Pray proceed, sir."

"Very well. Here is what I propose we do." As Tangeni drew the curtains across the static view of night-time London, Reardon craned his neck and peered high to the southwest, at Big Ben's clock face. The professor went on, "With the resources at our disposal, we are quite able to restore the giant furnace and steam engine which power my machine. All we require are steady supplies of fuel for the furnace—without petroleum and with little coal, wood will have to suffice—and plenty of water for the boiler. I suggest we dig a well to the fresh water beneath us. Anyone able to wield an axe should be put to cutting trees, preferably in the western forest away from the baryonyx."

He retrieved a notepad, its pages dry but ruffled by the damp, and a small pencil from his trouser pocket. While scribbling something, he muttered to himself before adding aloud, "You can guarantee my safety while I work in the factory, Verity?"

"I can. As many men as you need."

"Then by my reckoning, provided the wrench through time didn't inflict serious damage, and if those materials I mentioned are easily procurable, my machine should be in working order before the week is out." He licked his fingertip and flicked the page. "However, my

Harrison clock requires absolute accuracy. Its primary lens array cannot be damaged in any way. If that is intact, and I am able to initiate the influx and refraction of psammeticum energy, I believe we will have success, ladies and gentlemen—I mean friends," he corrected himself, lifted his chin proudly, then shut his notebook and put it back in his pocket. "Now, what else would you like to know?"

"What went wrong?" Embrey asked between sips of his brandy. "This talk of recreating the experiment is all well and good but how, for the love of God, did we wind up in the Cretaceous?"

Verity sat up. "Precisely. *That* is our conundrum, Professor. What's to stop your machine from behaving like a complete arse next time? You say we ought to have travelled back to 1901?" She motioned to the curtain and beyond. "Forgive us if we don't sprinkle confetti on your record, sir."

"Fair enough. But what choice is there?" Reardon shrugged one shoulder and held out his hand. "Within the parameters of its design, the machine is as accurate as I can possibly make it. I have no idea whatsoever why it veered so far off course. Interference from the storm perhaps. But the disparity between seven years and a hundred *million* years suggests time itself has some underlying property we have yet to comprehend. Fear not, though—I will divine it soon enough, perhaps after the next jump."

Embrey scoffed, "Very presumptuous, old boy. And if you don't mind me saying so, wrongheaded."

"Which part?"

"Restarting that mechanism without the foggiest idea of where we might end up. We'd be as well to stay here indefinitely—where we *know* there's food and water, where we have defensible buildings—as fling ourselves onto your temporal roulette again. Who knows when or where we'd find ourselves? Underwater? A billion years into the future? Or further into the past? In Genesis perhaps, inside a piping volcano?"

"Then you stay here, Embrey." Reardon swatted away the marquess's protest. "But as soon as my machine is in working order, I am making a second trip. And a third, and however many it takes me to reach 1901. Anyone who wishes to join me is welcome. Anyone else can pick his own grave."

A cheer from below deck set Verity ill-at-ease. She nervously picked at her nails. Suddenly, the problem was not a scientific one but rather a nebulous, cosmic gamble. Her colleagues had been right to invite Embrey in after all. He was frank and pragmatic. Reardon, on the other hand, now struck her as quite insane—a man railing against the forces that had wronged him in his past. Part Ahab, part Quixote, he was both their only chance of escape *and* their biggest liability.

A serious dilemma faced the camp, and every person would have to decide it for himself; trust Reardon's machine would work properly this time and return them to the twentieth century, or remain in prehistory forever, find a measure of solace in…whatever one found solacing in a world of bees and dinosaurs.

Her gaze set upon Embrey. He sipped his brandy. A distant roar silenced the cheers below.

Chapter 10

The God Spider

It felt strange after all these years of practising clandestine science to be giving an open tutorial on the inner workings of his Harrison clock, but even his friends had started to doubt his ability to return them to their own time. Today he would inspect every millimetre of the device and determine what, if anything, he needed to adjust in order to instigate a second time jump. Embrey's and Verity's objections were simply foolish. For castaways to remain stranded when they had a chance of returning home—whatever the risk—made absolutely no sense. They'd prefer to scratch a living among the deadliest predators the world had ever seen? Devolve into human scavengers? He'd give them a matter of weeks, at best.

No, the *Empress Matilda* had served her purpose in letting him identify the current geological era. Billy's book had also helped. Pinpointing 1908 A.D. after a 110-120 million year misfire might appear a far-fetched proposition but he believed utterly in the mechanics of his machine. Something external had affected the refraction process—some contaminant he'd overlooked, perhaps an atmospheric anomaly endemic to a storm environment. Had the charged air that night exacerbated the psammeticum reaction somehow, catalysed some kind of exponential energy shift?

It sure as hell wasn't *random,* as the others had conjectured. Science did not subscribe to randomness, and this machine was his masterpiece. The only way to determine the cause of the disparity was to repeat the experiment until it worked according to plan. And if it didn't…well, maybe it was God intervening after all. Maybe the Almighty could not allow him to unpick fate's cruel tapestry. Maybe his Lisa and Edmond could never…*maybe, maybe, maybe…*

He gritted his teeth and shook all doubt from his mind. A sickly whiff of burnt rubber and petrol made him gag as he led his entourage around the side of his factory to the front entrance. Embrey and Verity, both armed and alert, followed close behind. Six other aeronauts carried rifles.

When he reached the loading bay doors, a short man wearing a fancy waistcoat stepped out. "Ah, there you are, Professor. We've been waiting for you." Cecil recognized him from Agnes Polperro's retinue. He'd visited the factory for the inspection shortly before the time jump.

"Excuse me?" Thumbs in his waistcoat pockets, Cecil approached. "What the devil do you mean, skulking about inside my workplace? For God's *sake,* man, this place has to be off limits. Tell him, Verity."

She stepped forward with three of her men and stood akimbo. "He's right. I told you not to interfere in any way with Professor Reardon's machine. Now who's with—"

"Lieutenant Champlain," a woman's curt voice shot out from the shadowy interior, "nice of you to visit."

102

Agnes Polperro marched past her doorman, drawing her retinue of twelve well-dressed men with her onto the concrete outside. Verity faced her while looking askance at the men's vexed expressions. What on earth were they doing here? Why the unanimous frowns?

Embrey and the remaining aeronauts strode forward to even the odds.

"Miss Polperro, can we help you with something?" Verity adjusted her pith helmet. "I thought I made it quite clear this factory is under my jurisdiction."

"I daresay things have changed somewhat in your absence." The unpleasant schoolmarm nodded and whispered to Carswell, one of the drunken politicians who'd tried to hang Cecil that first night.

Cecil's lungs tightened. He gasped for air. Reliving those awful moments he'd endured at the end of a rope—throat warped shut, toes tingling, head swelling like a balloon—he began to shake. But the idea of his worst enemies invading his private sanctuary, the place he'd invested so much of himself these past six years, his dear and bittersweet perihelion, sparked his fury. "You bastards can all rot in hell!" He lunged for Verity's pistol and would have murdered Agnes Polperro and Carswell and anyone else whose face he recognised, had Verity not snatched the weapon away from him.

Embrey restrained him from behind. "Easy, Reardon. Take it easy, old boy. Now's not the time."

"*Right.* You'd better explain yourself in a hurry." Verity stepped toward Miss Polperro, their sharp gazes clashing like rapiers.

"Gladly. But I'd suggest you keep that crazed lunatic on a leash. He's a liability to himself and everyone around him."

"On the contrary, it's *you* who put those murderous thoughts in his head. All of you." Verity pointed angrily at the Whitehall gang. "You're bloody lucky I don't put the lot of you on trial for what you did to him. You snivelling pukes. Either step aside right now or give me good reason not to slake the professor's vengeance for him. Starting with you, Carswell, you pompous scum. I've a mind to put one between your rat eyes just for the hell of it."

Carswell's bushy eyebrows dropped and formed a V in the middle. He bared his teeth. Cecil felt oddly relieved that it wasn't quite himself against the world. With strong allies like Verity and Embrey at his side, maybe he could afford to calm down and rethink things a little.

"You'd better come with me." Miss Polperro crooked her finger.

"What for?"

"It changes everything. You'll see. But tread carefully—there is something extraordinary taking place here."

What could she mean? Something *more* extraordinary than his machine? The Whitehall gang parted while Miss Polperro led Cecil, Verity and Embrey into the heart of Cecil's creation—the giant, dormant cogs and the five cylinder steam engine, the Hillary magno-abacus resembling a miniature silver pipe organ, and the differentiator's U-shaped brass casing one could only reach from underneath whilst the machine was in motion. At least no one had found his Harrison clock yet.

The insufferable woman guided them into the work shed, through a maintenance door and into a corridor running eastward, adjacent to the machine. Wire mesh fencing provided no protection from hot vapour, and as the machine had been operating almost continuously for four years, Cecil hadn't ventured into this particular corridor during that time.

They walked another thirty feet past the final steam exhaust before Miss Polperro halted them at a secluded, bare-brick alcove he was certain he'd *never* seen before. "Well, here it is," she said. "Can any of you explain it?"

Cecil squeezed past her to gain an unobstructed view of…

"A spider's web?" Lord Embrey groaned. "You've found a glow-in-the-dark spider's web? Well, I think I speak for everyone here when I say, sod the tuffett and bugger the curds and whey."

Miss Polperro adjusted her thick-rimmed spectacles, then ran her fingers impatiently along the brick wall, over and over the same spot, clearly waiting for someone to cotton on to…whatever she'd seen in the web.

Verity shrugged and admitted she was at a loss. "I remember a lilac glow emitted in the run-up to the time jump… This web has the same colour. Unless that has some scientific significance…"

Confused, Cecil inspected the web at close range. Yes, the lilac coating was abnormal; no, it didn't worry him unduly. Residual energy traces lined various nooks and crannies higher up in the factory as well. So what on earth had Miss Polperro seen that he—

Wait. That can't be. No spider could…

"How closely have you inspected it?" he asked her.

She cracked a smug grin. "With magnifying glasses, spectrometer goggles, and the highest-powered microscope from your workshop. Their conclusion is beyond doubt."

He let the concept swim in his brain for a moment. There had to be some mistake—bureaucratic Leviacrum amateurs jumping to conclusions. Before he could swallow something this unlikely, he would have to perform his own rigorous tests. "You mean to tell me you didn't find a single—"

"Give us *some* credit, Professor," she said. "And if you don't believe me, scrutinize it at your leisure. It is unprecedented, and some of my colleagues believe it changes everything— your experiment, our so-called accidental destination, the prudence of us even attempting time travel again. They believe we must reassess our entire venture."

"And you?"

"I think we must take every precaution to ensure our next time jump is our last, at least until we can get to the bottom of this miraculous—and troubling—side-effect."

The more Cecil tried to compartmentalize her concerns, the more they threatened to flood his reasoning altogether. If the theory held up, it was potentially more startling than *time travel itself.* He clasped his hands on the back of his skull and tried to squeeze his elbows together.

"Oi, riddlers—stop speaking in code." Verity prodded Cecil out of his funk. "Spectro-whatsists? Magnifying micro-spiffy-ometers? What's got you both in such a muck-sweat?"

"Not my curds and whey comment, I pray?" Embrey shrugged.

As Cecil stepped back, the sound of his shoe tapping on the concrete echoed around the factory. He glanced round at his machine and then gazed up to the rickety platform on which he'd spent so much time watching, waiting for salvation, for the elusive combination to God's temporal lock. And now that he'd opened it, what *else* had he uncovered?

"Do either of you believe in God?" Miss Polperro asked his companions.

They both nodded.

"But have you ever seen Him, heard His voice?"

"Not sober," replied Embrey.

"Never," said Verity.

His hands trembling for the first time in a long time, Cecil pulled out his pipe, then sheepishly put it back in his pocket.

Miss Polperro faced the three of them, her cruel features quivering. "It is our contention that science has surpassed its limit here." Her lip and chin trembled. "And that we may have just found evidence…of the divine."

Embrey and Verity shared a puzzled look.

No, that superstitious angle probably wasn't the most fecund way to introduce a discovery like this. "Or let us put it a different way," Cecil said. "Somewhere in this factory is the most extraordinary spider ever born—"

"Or *created*," countered Agnes Polperro.

"My friends, this web appears to be flawless. Not just to the naked eye but, insofar as they have ascertained, irreducibly flawless. And as it must have been created *since* the time jump—the flood would have washed it away otherwise—it appears time travel has affected this spider in a most profound way." He roved his fingers over the lilac thread, careful not to touch. "It has inspired him to spin an infinitesimally perfect web."

Chapter 11

Precious Pieces

"Nothing anyone says will change your mind, I take it?" Verity didn't need an answer from Reardon, and none came. She'd thought him a little eccentric before, even self-absorbed, but there was a lot more to it than that. No one else seemed to realise how damaged he really was—whenever he mentioned his wife and son it was with a flippant matter-of-factness, as though he spoke with them daily. The others seemed to mistake it for an odd quirk, a side of his dotty professorial charm. Perhaps it took another wounded, driven soul to recognise his torment. But she'd honoured Bernie by becoming the best aeronaut she could possibly be, a reasonable enough pursuit. And perhaps she might one day come to terms with a world without her. Perhaps. Reardon, though, could *never* say goodbye to his loved ones, heal, and move on in the natural way. Without knowing how he would achieve it, he was bound on this relentless, messianic quest the way a clock hand spins in pursuit of its elusive destination.

The sun beat down on his unkempt silver hair, and he had to shade his eyes with a fixed salute. She knelt at his side in the middle of the street and handed him her pith helmet.

"Thank you." He pointed to his toolbox. "Would you hand me a five-eighths spanner from the rack?"

She did so. But the labyrinthine design of his Harrison clock didn't make a lick of sense to her. Every tiny cog and shaft from its brass innards was spread on the blanket before them. Nothing individually, these were nonetheless the components of a bona fide miracle.

A miracle. But what had Reardon really tapped into with time travel? The mysterious spider's web was beyond science, Miss Polperro had said, beyond even the professor's understanding. Was there actually a divine force at work here, or was Briory's godless theory correct and the temporal explosion had simply misfired somehow, copying that web pattern in its most efficient geometric form—perfection?

Either explanation opened a can of worms. If it was divine, why hadn't God intervened further and saved dozens of lives? Why leave only a cryptic clue of His presence? And why had He guided them to the Cretaceous? More questions than answers.

If this was all a trick of science, what undiscovered forces had conspired to *deliberately* reshape the web that way? Nothing infinitesimally perfect could be an accident. Even she knew that. So why couldn't she subscribe to Miss Polperro's doom-mongering? The machine was dangerous, not just to the camp but to space and time itself. Should she ban Reardon from using it again, or, as someone else had suggested, destroy the infernal thing once and for all?

While kneeling beside him, watching him reassemble complex mirror arrays and energy conductors as though he were piecing together a jigsaw already complete in his mind, she began to see the conundrum from Reardon's point of view.

If one can travel through time, fate needn't be absolute.

An illicit spark blazed through the fog of her memory and, for one breathless moment, Bernie was alive and well somewhere in the world...in 1908. By dint of Verity's temporal intervention, Bernie could avoid the fire in Benguela and live on to a ripe old age. Fate be damned! The idea left her shivery, excited and craving more...

I could bring Amyn *back, as well! My beautiful fiancé...have our wedding after all. And then Captain Naismith. I could bring them all to England, keep them out of harm's way. By God, Reardon's right! To not try would be the real folly.*

"Professor, I think I've made my decision." She sat up straight.

He grunted in reply, without looking up.

Verity went on excitedly, "If you can get a handle on navigating through time, sir. If you manage to solve this great puzzle of when-and-why, I am with you. These iniquities in fate's design *deserve* to be undone. To hell with the consequences! Our first duty is to those we love, to safeguard their lives against all malign forces, even death. The way I see it, God has allowed you to invent this great unraveller. Ergo, the laws of fate are not sacrosanct. I'd say using it for love is more than justifiable."

"Indeed." He snatched a glimpse of her while wiping his brow, then resumed his work. "Everything within our power. We'll never be complete if we don't try. Let God stop it if He must." Reardon sounded like he was reciting a mantra. "I'm glad you're seeing it my way, Verity. If only the others had your vision."

111

Not likely. The crescent line of chairs in the middle of the road, where Parliament Street intersected Bridge Street, was almost empty. Polperro's posse was not enjoying the sunshine this afternoon. A group of six or seven men in shirtsleeves was busy extracting useable furniture and perishables from the northernmost damaged houses before the structures collapsed altogether. Miss Polperro had summoned her top minions—as Embrey called them—including Carswell, Delaney and four of her Leviacrum retinue for an animated powwow in the shade of the gentlemen's club. The discussion could very well be harmless and confined to the day-to-day running of the camp, but Verity didn't like the constant glances in her direction or the schoolmarm's angry finger-wagging at her colleagues.

Thank God Djimon and the others are here.

Her aeronauts were playing cards on the sun-baked kerb. In the centre of them, Embrey appeared out of place in his white vest and expensive trousers. His blond hair seemed to bleach more with each afternoon. Soon he would look almost albino. A dashing, infuriating, prehistoric albino…who blew at gin rummy.

"Why don't you take a walk with him? It would serve our cause immensely if you two could cease hostilities." Reardon's impertinence poured out so matter-of-factly, she almost called to Embrey there and then. "Come now," he said, "you cannot play counterparts forever. Sooner or later, clockwork requires each piece to accept its nature or break. Hearts are no different."

"I beg your pardon?"

"Pass me that glass polisher?" The professor winked and then whistled a tune to himself.

112

The downright cheek. If only to escape his weirdness, Verity snatched her helmet from him and left. But rather than head back to the *Empress,* she veered toward the card game and, after fanning her hot flush, looked away and blurted out, "Care to take a walk, Embrey?"

She cringed and vowed to undo those words with all the other wrongs she'd get to right with the machine—

"Absolutely." Ignoring boos and taunts from the mirthful aeronauts, Embrey leapt to his feet and offered her the way. "Ladies first."

This is a mistake already. "We need to get a few things straight—" she waited until they were out of earshot of her men, "—and I've something crucial to ask you."

"Likewise. It's time we cleared the air, Miss Champlain."

A cold, distant remark. "Yes it is...Lord Embrey." *Ugh.* Despite what she wanted to ask him about his father, a sore part of her couldn't swallow that barbed surname. Not now. Not ever.

They headed northwest, by the steam car wreckage and the crumbling terrace Miss Polperro's men had just finished looting. Sections of the quagmire beyond, where the Thames water had drained into the soil, were now brick dry, a kind of murky green-grey colour. The top of the tree-line fidgeted, and she thought she heard crowing noises coming from the forest.

"So what would you like to ask?" Embrey's well-defined upper body muscles were glazed with perspiration, while a tuft of blond chest hair teased her from beneath the low neck of his vest. A scar ran across his right pectoral muscle and down toward his ribs. Painful. And if she wasn't mistaken, an animal's claw had

113

inflicted that injury. A number of her comrades had succumbed to wildlife attacks in Africa over the years.

"A polo souvenir?" She immediately regretted the jibe.

He eyed her quizzically, but seemed more amused than insulted. "Colca Canyon, Peru."

"Peru? That's the other side of the world. What on earth were you doing there?"

"Exploring with my uncle and a few of my old Oxford chums. We found an ancient trail to a derelict settlement—not one of our more prodigious finds, if I'm perfectly honest." He snorted a laugh. "You look at me as though I'd be lost outside the drawing room without a compass."

Verity smiled. "The thought had occurred to me. So how exactly were you wounded?"

"I had a slight culinary disagreement with a giant condor."

"Disagreement?"

"Yes. He tried to steal my supper. His manners needed mending."

"And what happened?"

"He mended mine instead." Embrey ran his finger down his scar, all the way from collar to hip. "So you can see why I don't much care for anything that flies. Present company accepted, of course."

Interesting. He's more adventurous than I thought.

"My sister visited South America once—Brazil, I think—with the bluecoats. The Amazon scared the life out of her. Insects as big as kites. Apparently some parts of the river are so wide it's more like crossing a sea."

"Very true. This place seems like Kew Gardens and its duck pond in comparison." He paused, cleared his throat. "Miss Champlain, I'd just like to say, I'm very sorry for your loss. The Benguela attack was despicable, and I can assure you, despite what you might have heard, that neither my family nor myself had anything to do with it."

"Oh." So he wanted to exonerate himself once and for all while she was in a pliable mood, did he? Well, in that case he had some fancy talking to do. He'd answered her question, but it would take a lot more than that—the evidence against his father and uncle had been damning. "Tangeni said you'd try to convince me sooner or later." Embrey's brow stitched, as if her tone had been too harsh and she'd wounded him. "He also said I should listen," she added.

"Aye, a rare fellow, that Tangeni." But to her disappointment, he didn't follow up. Instead, he narrowed his glazed eyes and then looked away to hide his grief. He seemed so lonely, so sad, she hadn't the heart to press him further just yet. But that time would come.

"Hey, speaking of adventures, I met Quatermain once." She tugged his vest.

"Really?" He blinked rapidly. "Pray tell."

"Two summers ago he was leading an expedition into Kukuanaland. We flew over on our way to supply a team of mineral surveyors when he lit a distress lamp. One of his trail guides was crippled with fever, so we had to land and take him back to hospital."

"Wasn't contagious, I hope."

"No. And the best part is…the guide had performed heroics along the way…saved a friend of Quatermain's. And so Quatermain gave him a parting gift. In case the guide didn't survive, we were to pass the gift on to his family. You'll never guess what it was."

"Not a diamond the size of a cricket ball, by chance?"

Verity halted him. "How in God's name did you know that?"

"I'm good." Rubbing his stubble, he teased her with a smug-but-really-rather-cute pout. "And it made all the papers in London."

"No joking?"

"No." Embrey thumbed his braces, seemed more boy than man. Verity's heart warmed. "To English ears, any tale involving Quatermain or Horace Holly is like rumours of Heracles's exploits to the ancient Greeks. Storytelling ambrosia. And when King Solomon's *diamonds* are involved—"

"I know." She tipped her helmet back and suddenly felt more exposed than she was comfortable with. *To hell with comfort. This concerns Quatermain.* "It was all we could talk about for weeks after. Tangeni even traded with him—gave Quatermain a spare canteen in exchange for one of his rifle bullets. I don't know how the deuce he plucked the courage to do that."

"Did you speak to him?"

Verity leaned in and whispered in his ear, "Don't tell anyone, but I went as weak as a schoolgirl with a crush." The heady excitement of being this close to him, close enough to taste his natural, intoxicating scent, dizzied her for a moment.

He whispered back, "What did you say?"

"That I…that I…"

"That you what?"

"That I loved—"

116

A crash of thunder ripped them apart, spun them toward the last building on Parliament Street. Thick dust jets shot out of the windows and open crevices while the structure collapsed. First the rear, then the upper north wall caved in with a rumble. Finally, the entire front of the building buckled and spilled forward onto the road, its mammoth roar making Verity cover her ears. She flinched and stumbled back.

They watched as the dust and debris fizzed out and settled on the asphalt and the guts of the building were laid bare. Men came running. One or two rummaged through the rubble to reach three or four crushed bodies. Embrey ran to help them. The other men pointed away toward the northwest tree-line, where the upper branches swayed violently. One gent ran back to camp, waving his arms in distress.

Verity's vision blurred. Her mouth went dry. *Metal?* Why did her saliva taste of…metal? A red fingertip after brushing her lips suggested she'd bit her tongue. Then why did—?

She traced a line of blood up to her nose, then up her nose to her brow. Finally she located an aching gash, where the brim of her helmet should have been if she hadn't tipped it back. The wound bled slowly but constantly. She didn't have the strength or the wherewithal to cry for help. Only a memory of strolling about the quarterdeck seemed to keep her from falling.

Suddenly her eyes filled with diamonds, and she lost consciousness.

Too many surprises all at once caught up with Embrey as he sat on the kerb near Reardon's clock parts and rubbed his tired eyes. Four aeronauts kept vigil around the professor, while one rushed to the *Empress* for bandages and antiseptic ointment. Djimon stayed with Verity in the shade outside the factory. Luckily, she'd come round almost right away after fainting, and Embrey had nursed her in his arms until her men had arrived. How *intimate* they'd become in so short a time. That talk of Quatermain had cut through their animosity nicely. But how? Why was she so well disposed to him all of a sudden? Because he'd saved her life and she his? Or perhaps Reardon and Tangeni had talked some sense into her after all, made her realise that the British legal system had more holes than a sinking sloop, that his family *hadn't* had a hand in her sister's death.

Whatever the reason, he loved the change in her. Beneath the prickly Amazon warrior, Verity Champlain had a lasting crush on Quatermain, and the way she'd tugged at his vest, like a little girl wanting to spill a secret—she had a vibrant, playful side he'd like to see more of. When she recovered he would see about resuming their conversation. If she didn't turn on him again, that was. But in any event, he would not allow a woman who enjoyed adventuring as much as he did to slip through his fingers. *No, ma'am.*

"What's this talk of a royal found in the rubble, old chap?" Reardon called over.

Yawning, Embrey looked up into the professor's intense gaze. "That's correct. Carswell insists we've found the Duke of Kent. His face was smashed and he's dressed casually, but Carswell recognized two of the other men from the duke's royal entourage. They all died during the time jump. We haven't found them until now because they'd been buried in a collapsed upper room.

118

Died drinking port, apparently. Not the worst way to go."

Reardon blinked twice and then returned to his work.

"How goes it, Professor?"

"Like clockwork."

"Anything I can help you with?"

"No."

"Anything I can get you? A beverage? A bite to eat?"

"No."

"Want to be left alone, huh."

Reardon grunted.

Cantankerous old bugger. Embrey put on the spectrometer goggles he'd borrowed from the workshop, and lay back on the concrete, feeling wonderfully superfluous. A flock of pterosaurs streaked in front of the sun, their silhouettes no bigger than dragonflies—far, far above—and they didn't appear to be circling. Nothing to worry about. He folded his arms behind his head, closed his eyes and soaked up the sun's warmth.

An hour or so had passed, judging from the sun's shifted position in the sky. Reardon was still hard at work under the parasol they'd erected, adjusting his mirrors and lenses, checking the angles of sunlight refracting through his various prisms. At least he'd cobbled the pieces together into a few substantial parts now—sizeable, complex mechanisms. One resembled a large Leonardo Da Vinci cryptex filled with several long shafts and rotating lenses. When the professor lifted it, its insides appeared to form a beautiful, multi-chambered kaleidoscope.

Embrey sat up, yawned and stretched. He saw no sign of Verity. She'd probably returned to her cabin on the ship. He would visit her presently. Polperro's posse had already laid the five new corpses on Speaker's Green and was busy digging fresh graves. How many more would there be? Despite Reardon's unflappable confidence in his machine, could it *ever* whisk them through time with any degree of accuracy? The professor maintained the first mis-jump was nothing more than a hiccup, but Embrey and Verity had seen his face turn white when confronted with the inexplicable spider's web. Garrett Embrey was no scientist. Whom, then, should he defer to? The man who'd invented time travel, or the woman whose job it had been to make sure *he* didn't invent time travel?

Both were barking mad.

It's all beyond me. I'd better consult with Verity and Tangeni instead. He grinned. *Yes, sharing a cabin with the captain might at least help my...perspective.*

He spun at the sound of a high-pitched whistle. But where exactly had it—

"Lord Embrey! Protect the professor!" one of the aeronauts yelled from Speaker's Green. "We're under attack!"

Polperro's posse fled from what looked like multi-coloured streaks darting about on the lawn. Several inhuman shrieks wrenched him to full alert. He drew his steam-pistols and shielded Reardon, who picked up his own rifle. The four aeronauts formed a protective line.

"Anything comes this way, kill it." Embrey aimed his weapons.

A creature dashed across the street, as fast as a dog after a fleeing man. It had the general shape and profile of a tyrannosaur, but it was much smaller, about the size of a large wolf. Colourful feathers on its arms, neck and long tail gave it a tropical, birdlike appearance. The bugger attacked with ferocity. Its size belied a hugely powerful musculature. After it bit into the man's throat, ripping his windpipe out with a single crunch, Embrey shared a trepidatious look with his Africans colleagues. He double-checked the water-acid canisters for both his pistols.

"What the hell is it? Some kind of pack hunter? *Hey*—" Reardon had to stop his five bodyguards from stepping back any further and trampling his machine parts. One of the Africans knocked the parasol over instead. "Somebody fire a shot," the professor said. "Alert the rest of the crew. These civilians are unarmed."

He was right. Embrey fired into the air. Two of the dinosaurs dragged a human body from the lawn onto the street, and began squabbling over it. A third took advantage of the kerfuffle, sinking its sickle-like claw and razor teeth into one of the Duke of Kent's retinue. Perhaps even the duke himself.

Embrey gagged. A volley of gunfire erupted from the *Empress's* direction moments before Reardon swivelled him northward. A hurtful shriek rang in his ears as two feathered predators bore down on them from behind. He aimed and fired both his pistols. One dinosaur fell dead on the cobblestone. The other barged into the machine parts while Reardon and an aeronaut dove out of the way. Its claw caught the arm of a standing African, gouging a deep wound. Embrey shot into the feathers on its spine and hurried away from its thrashing limbs and death-throe shrieks. All six men finished it.

121

Another dinosaur leapt from out of nowhere, cleaving the injured man's neck as it landed on him. He tore fistfuls of feathers but to no avail. By the time they killed the beast, it had bitten through the poor aeronaut's skull.

"Son of a *bitch*." They were too exposed out here. If a dinosaur pack attacked in full force, the situation would be hopeless. "Come on, we must get indoors." He yanked Reardon toward the factory but the professor wouldn't budge.

"Stop it, man. For God's sake, is your brain smogged?"

Reardon stood his ground, cocked his rifle, glancing every which way—panic jerked him round and round.

"Men, we don't have time for this, and we can't afford to lose him." Embrey glared at the professor. "Take him by force."

"Yes, sir."

Two of the aeronauts frog-marched him off the street, while the third rushed to fold the blanket over Reardon's clock pieces. No sooner had he covered the first contraption than the sun-baked road darkened and a giant pterosaur swooped on top of him. The man tried to fling the blanket and its contents out of reach but only succeeded in spilling them.

"*No.*" Embrey shot twice but the monstrous flier flapped its wings. Dust and rock pellets hit like a blizzard, forcing him to shield his face.

A second pterosaur glided low over the rooftops opposite, its malign caws filling London with dread. Reardon tried his darnedest to break free and save his clock, but the aeronauts held him firm. "You stupid sod," Embrey scolded him. "We *need* you, damn you. We need you alive."

"But my Harrison clock! I'll never be able to find them without it. Get off me, you heathen bastards!"

The first pterosaur skipped away as several rifle shots sounded from the north. It snatched the mauled aeronaut up in its beak and rose into the air, dropping the blanket onto the street. The force of its wings kicked up a storm. Embrey winced as the clock parts bounced away and clattered on the concrete.

Immediately, a pack of feathered dinosaurs assailed the pterosaur. They ripped its wings and brought it down writhing on its back. One last sickening shriek faded to a pitiful groan. The melee ended outside the gentlemen's club, where the bipedal carnivores gathered for an avian smorgasbord.

Stunned, Embrey crept out to retrieve the clock parts. After Reardon, they were all that mattered. The hiss of Billy's tri-wheel car approached from the north. Kibo drove. Tangeni leaned out of the passenger side, waving frantically.

At me? What on earth has happened now?

Embrey checked behind him but the feathered predators were all ensconced in their feast at the far end of the street.

Just a greeting, then.

He collected the first of the clock parts. Tangeni cupped his hands to his mouth and yelled something unintelligible—he waved again, but this time it seemed to darken the entire sky. Embrey's blood iced and he glanced up.

The second pterosaur landed ten yards away and snatched up the shiny kaleidoscopic cylinder in its talon.

God, no. He had to shield his face from the hurricane whipped up by its wings. Before he could aim and shoot, the bastard was airborne and flying south, its grip on their future unyielding.

"Bring it down! What the hell are you waiting for?" Reardon broke free from the aeronauts. He took a snapshot with his rifle and missed. Embrey's pistols were empty, so he grabbed one of the aeronaut's rifles and tried to pip the burglar before it veered over the rooftops, out of sight...

Too late.

"Oh, Christ, that's it now. Lisa and Edmond! I've lost them. We're all lost. We're all buggered. You stupid bastards have gone and dug our graves. We're buggered, buggered, bug—"

"Professor, *shut up.* You're giving me a headache." Embrey turned and sprinted for the tri-wheel car and said to Tangeni, "It's turned east. We have to catch it."

"Who's the best shot with a rifle?"

"I am." Jostling his friend aside, Embrey dove onto the passenger seat and ordered the driver, "Head east, Kibo—as fast as this heap will go. Everything depends on it."

"On my way."

Under Kibo's control the car gathered steam far quicker than Billy's father had accelerated it that night during the storm. It reached upwards of twenty miles an hour as they passed parallel to the *Empress*, and still it sped up. Kibo had mentioned he used to drive racers on the European circuits. He more than proved it.

The pterosaur circled over the rocky escarpment, the metallic glint still evident in its right talon. *Christ, if it made for the ocean...*

"Where to?" Kibo kept his eye out for rocks on the otherwise flat, grassy terrain, glancing skyward only rarely.

"East. No, northeast. It's heading for the coast. Make for the bottleneck through the forest. I'll have to take a shot from the cliff. And hurry!"

"Aye, sir."

Though the pterosaur was capable of much higher speeds, it flew into the wind, which evened the odds for the steam-powered tri-wheel. Twenty feet before the cliff, Embrey yelled for Kibo to stop. Rifle cocked and warm in his grip, he jumped out and took aim, compensating for the wind speed and direction while he rested the barrel on the roof of the car. *Hell fire.* The sun was in his eyes.

He fiddled the knob on the side of his spectrometer goggles until the lenses tinted enough to quell the sun's glare. *Better.* He loosened his shoulders and crouched. The flier had climbed sharply. Four hundred feet now, at least.

"Winner's grace…pips the ace." His father's shooting mantra.

The deep inhale and cool, prolonged exhale. The smooth adjustments. Not just knowing but *feeling* the right moment to squeeze the trigger, the way a snake senses its time to strike…

Crack!

He sucked in a hopeful gasp and held it. A few seconds later, the pterosaur jerked, fell limp from the sky and plummeted.

Kibo gave a cheer. "*Omafele atatu, omafele anee.* And in strong *omhepo*…strong wind. That was the best shot I ever saw."

But Embrey's own celebration fell bitterly with the pterosaur. He watched in horror as Reardon's cylinder plopped into the lake, over three hundred feet offshore. The monstrous dinosaur splashed on top of it, and both quickly sank from sight.

Chapter 12

Snakes and Ladders

Verity would never have left the camp so soon after such a devastating attack had there been any other choice. A further seven men had died, a half dozen more were injured, and with the smell of blood in the air London would surely attract other dinosaurs on the hunt. Three separate species had now attacked, all of them deadly in their own ways. The latest was arguably the most dangerous of all—its silent approach and small, agile shape gave it an immediate advantage over anyone trying to survive among the Westminster ruins.

"Them were dromaeosaurus—pack hunters from t' late Cretaceous Period." Billy scanned the page in his book. "We should correct that last part, shouldn't we? The name means 'running lizard'. First 'un were discovered in 1864 durin' a Leviacrum-sponsored expedition to Canada. Dromaeosaurs were mainly scavengers but sometimes brought down much bigger prey."

"As we saw." Embrey, wearing only long-johns and a vest, stepped into the canvas diving suit, his chiselled, sensational upper body on display for Verity and the rest of the crew. She evaded his glance. "What are those fliers called again, Billy?" he asked. "Hat shops? Jodhpur tricks?"

The boy laughed. "Hatzegopteryx."

"That's the one. And its fossils were found in Romania?"

"Yeah. 1902."

"A mite far from their nest, wouldn't you say, Professor?"

Reardon looked up from his notebook. "Not necessarily. Migratory birds often cross oceans and continents, and we don't know where the Hatzegopteryx goes to nest. Just because a pterosaur fossil was found in one place doesn't mean the species is endemic to that region. For all we know, they're Londoners like us."

She frowned. *Londoners. But for how long?* This handful of crumbling buildings would not protect Polperro's posse indefinitely. So why on earth were they being so stubborn? Verity had invited them to reside on the *Empress* indefinitely, under armed protection. But the insufferable schoolmarm and her lickspittle cronies had opted to stay behind during this crucial flight. It made no sense, and yet—

"Miss Polperro, what do you plan to do in the event of another attack?" Verity asked.

The de facto lady Prime Minister stood at the ladder next to Kincaid, the elderly statesman who appeared to be advising her. "We were just discussing that, Lieutenant. If you would be so good as to lend us five or six of your men, we could—"

"Regretfully, no. I'm sorry, but we will require every spare hand to man the capstans and the winch. The diving bell is a tremendous weight, and we are already under-manned."

Miss Polperro closed her parasol and, nose upturned, looked askance at Verity. "As many rifles as you can spare, then? Woe is us indeed if we can't defend London at all in your absence. I understand you have a sizeable arsenal on board?"

"Sufficient, nothing more."

She's plotting something. First she refuses the safety of the ship, now she wants our weapons? How daft does she think I am?

"You can have two rifles," Verity offered reluctantly, "but I strongly urge you to reconsider moving into the fo'c'sle. It might be cramped down there, but at least you will have a crew of armed aeronauts watching over you. We can always make other arrangements upon our return. What do you say, ma'am?"

"We will take the rifles, thank you." Miss Polperro's instant smile was too polite, too pleasant for the occasion. The woman had just made a life-or-death decision and had erred on the side of risk. What did she and her cronies have up their sleeves? Did it have anything to do with the pious whisperings Mr. Briory had reported?

"Very well. But before we leave, might I enquire as to your position on the spider web phenomenon? Rumour has it some of your people are opposed to any further time travel attempts, that they would even try to prevent Professor Reardon from restoring his machine. Is this true?"

Kincaid stepped forward, chest-first. "We believe Reardon is meddling with primal forces beyond his ken." His voice shook with old age, and Verity felt a little sorry for him. "The spider's web is a message from the Almighty, of that there can be no doubt. But the purpose of that message is ambiguous, and therefore we must not be dogmatic. As for undoing Reardon's folly, I uphold your right to at least try. But that is my opinion, Miss Champlain, and I am neither scientist nor priest."

Verity nodded appreciatively. "And you, Miss Polperro? Where do you stand?"

"Where the wind changes, as always." She turned sharply, handed Kincaid her parasol, and climbed down the ladder without another word.

Icy bitch.

Kincaid bowed to Verity. "Good day, miss, and good luck to you."

"Thank you, sir. I wish our situation were more amenable. Would you like assistance climbing the ladder?" She called Tangeni over but winced when the Namibian hobbled on his sprained ankle.

"Thank you kindly, no," Kincaid replied. "I've scaled plenty of rigging in my days. Eighty-one and still going strong—"

She didn't catch his last remark and instead whispered to Tangeni, "Sod them if they think I'm giving them weapons. And we'll send four men to guard the factory, not two."

"And leave ourselves shorthanded?"

"We'll manage. I just don't trust that Whitehall rabble, not after the lynching party. Send four."

"Aye, Captain."

Watching Billy, Reardon and Briory potter around the diving equipment laid out for Embrey's instruction on the quarterdeck, hearing them joke and laugh at the marquess's ungainly appearance, was a little disconcerting. Little did they know how dangerous deep sea diving was *without* the prehistoric factor. The only other qualified diver in her crew, Tangeni would have been her only choice as diving partner had he not been injured—a sprained ankle was one of the worst possible handicaps under all that weight—but Embrey was a fine athlete and an excellent swimmer, or so he claimed. How would he fare in her domain, where charm meant nothing and life or death could be decided by a single twitch upon the thread?

Tangeni and Djimon would prepare him well, at least. And he *had* given them this chance with arguably the most crucial shot in the history of gunfire.

She shrugged and then ordered the pilot, "Northeast heading. Kibo saw where the bird fell. He will relieve you presently."

"Yes, *Eembu*…Captain."

"Embrey," she shouted. "After you, sir. It's time we took a dip."

"What the deuce…? Upon my word, this thing would sink Poseidon to the depths." He had never worn anything so ridiculously heavy in his life. The combined weight of his diving suit, boots, ballast weights and helmet was the equivalent of wearing another man on his back—an especially fat and bone-idle one at that.

In her unflattering, custom-sized waterproof suit and her smaller boots, Verity appeared calm and professional. Too much of both. Embrey's nerves were already frayed, his knees aquiver whenever the bell groaned under the rising pressure. How deep were they now? Two hundred feet. Maybe more. No longer a light sapphire, the water in the moon pool and through the porthole windows was grim, blue-green and littered with plankton.

"You ready, Lord Embrey?" Djimon madly wound the dynamo until the hull lights blazed on. "Remember, keep your helmet upright at all times. Think of it as an empty cup filled with air, held upside down in the water. Tip it too far to the side and—"

"I get the general idea, old boy. How do we return to the bell afterward?"

"Tug your tether line." Verity demonstrated with her own. "And whatever happens—*whatever* happens—for God's sake, follow my lead."

"Yes, *ma'am*."

Her grave head shake killed his nervous humour. He peered into the moon pool and glimpsed a four-foot-long fish dart undercover behind a forest of lithe, giant fronds. The lake bottom, neither sandy nor silty as he'd hoped, instead rose and fell craggily, a kind of volcanic rock sharp enough to cut him to ribbons should he slip. Muted colours dotted the shelves and crannies, while a school of spotted eels, each over a fathom's length, slithered up from a crevice and shot away from the bell's descent.

The scale of this prehistoric underwater world dawned on him in blunt jabs to his sense of the absurd. He recalled the startling creatures young Billy had described from his book—leviathans with names he couldn't remember, didn't want to remember. Their measurements were enough.

Verity sat on the moon pool's brass rim and tapped his shoulder. "Embrey, before we go…" her unblinking gaze appeared softer somehow, more exposed, "…I'd like to thank you for volunteering. Very brave."

Well, well.

"Be careful down there. I…we'd all be glad if you made it back in one piece," she added hurriedly.

"So would I." He rested his shivering hand on hers. So cold. So soft. So…unexpected. A thrilling wave curled through him. He felt he could shrug his gear off with a single breath if he should see her in peril, as though it were no more than a rain cloak. He'd never thought of her as vulnerable before. On the contrary, she was the flintiest woman he'd ever met. Where had this sudden urge to throw himself in harm's way for her come from?

"*Enda nawa*, Djimon," she said.

The cool African handed her a helmet. "Hurry back, *Eembu*."

"Drinks are on me later," Embrey said feebly.

Djimon clanked Embrey's helmet into place and knocked on the dome to signify it was ready. The sudden isolation slivered, as though his brain were physically imbibing a new experience. He'd skin dived in the Mediterranean before, even sat in a prototype moon rocket in its hangar as a youngster, but he'd never felt quite so…encapsulated. As Djimon helped him slide into the moon pool, the quickening *whuh, whuh* of his breaths seemed as alien to him as the seascape below.

The cold hit. He clenched from head to toe, but the fear of where he was going to land held his eyes wide open. He watched the sharp terrain as he sank. A few feet that way, no *that* way… Being lowered like a worm on a hook wasn't quite how he'd imagined it beforehand.

His boots settled on a solid ledge. He stumbled forward but remembered to hold his head upright. Verity landed several yards to his left and immediately pointed him toward an hourglass-shaped crevasse ahead.

The *Empress's* spotters had glimpsed something resembling a wingtip on the other side of that gap. It might be a long shot—the lake bed was murky at best, tough to discern when viewed from the surface—but he was certain the Hatzegopteryx had sunk in this vicinity.

He overstepped his first stride and ended up hopping sideways to keep balance. Verity wagged her finger at him, then demonstrated the correct walking posture—to lean forward, head ever-so-slightly bowed, and take unambitious, almost shuffling steps. He copied and gained proficiency in no time.

They leapt across the neck of the hourglass and, barely lit by the bell's lights, pressed on across a flat ledge. Towering stalks appeared on the edges of darkness, their bulbous fronds wavering as though to some ancient aquatic rhythm. Embrey's pulse hammered when he realized his own shadow was blackening his path. He tapped Verity on the shoulder, then pointed to the pack of flares in her belt. She lit one and tossed it at the forest.

A colossal form blazed into view among the shoots less than thirty feet ahead. Embrey saw its sharp teeth first—big and curved as Persian daggers. Endless rows of them. He recoiled too quickly and head butted the back of his helmet. Shock, not pain pulsed wetly through his skull. The creature didn't move from its place of ambush and neither he nor Verity shifted a step to encourage it. *Christ*, it's crocodilian jaws alone, partially agape and waiting, had to be well over ten feet long. Resembling a shorter-and-thicker-necked plesiosaur, it had four large paddle-like limbs and a short tail. But that mouth—unhinged—appeared ready to swallow the flare's light entirely.

Who moves first? Who dares?

Billy would have a name for this leviathan. Billy had the dinosaur bible. Well, Embrey had a name for it too. Several unrepeatable names hurtling around with hot gasps inside his helmet.

The cold seeped into him anew while they stood. A school of small fish flittered close, swirling twice around the flare before they seemed to sense danger and dashed for the cover of darkness. Still the dinosaur waited, its tail wafting gently. Several tiny fish picked at its giant teeth and gums—the brashest scavengers Embrey had ever witnessed. But the predator didn't seem to mind…rather, it appeared to *enjoy* the attention, its paddles twitching as though it were ticklish.

Its tail swatted to one side and he flinched, fearing the giant was about to rouse. He spied a metallic glint on the rock behind it instead.

Reardon's clock!

He nudged Verity and she acknowledged the discovery with a scowl and a nod.

Your move, Captain.

The flare faded and died before Embrey had a chance to swallow. A net of nightmares descended upon the lake bed. He tried to make out the monster's shape but couldn't. Through the blackness, dread in the deep grew both infinite and intimately close.

Verity?

Suddenly, their dilemma intensified tenfold. If they retreated now, the waiting giant might change its mind and kill them. If they stayed put, hoping it would leave, they may not see it come or go, and the wait might be indefinite. Would that he could hear Verity's thoughts right now. This was her domain after all.

She lit a second flare and tossed it away to their right. Heart in mouth, he watched her creep in the opposite direction, over twenty feet to one of the massive stalks. Thereon she flanked the leviathan under cover, inching toward the mechanism from shoot to shoot. But her oxygen hose pulled tight against the stalks. It scraped away a lather of green mulch, and he feared either the monster would react or the action might saw through the delicate plants, toppling them *onto* the beast.

Still the predator didn't move. Embrey ducked under Verity's hose as it pulled tight across him. She was at the end of its tether. Had she reached the clock mechanism in time? Indeed, could she even see it?

Another flare blazed inside the forest, near the dinosaur's hind paddle. *Please know what you're doing, Verity.* She tossed it away from the monster.

Before it landed, the lake burst to life. Dozens of large coin-shaped fish, each almost ten feet long, wrenched the stalks apart, barely avoiding Verity's taut hose. Embrey kept low but found himself wheeling backward in the wake of a stupendous current.

The leviathan shot out after the coin fish and vanished.

He pressed his hand to the iron weight over his heart. "Verity, where are you? What have you done?" A part of him knew it hadn't been an accident—she had to have tossed the flare deliberately at the fish, to incite this chase—but it was no less reckless, and he would give her a piece of his mind when they returned to the bell. "Whatever happens, follow my lead", she'd told him. *Bloody stupid.*

He took her advice and guided himself using her line. She almost bumped into him carrying Reardon's kaleidoscope, her blasé wink reminding him that while he was out of his depth, Verity Champlain most assuredly wasn't.

Thank you, God, on all counts.

To his surprise, she tugged him back into the forest and bade him follow her to a small glade where the latest flare had landed. She lit another.

As it fell, a flat rectangular shape glimmered on the jagged rock. Overgrown and a little discoloured, it appeared to be made of...but no, that was impossible.

He looked at Verity. She gazed back with no answer. But there *had* to be an answer.

Where the deuce had a metal panel that big come from?

"Another six! Luck smiles on me today." Reardon moved his counter up the Snakes and Ladders board, barely missing the head of a big serpent that would have taken him back to square one.

"Bloody rigged, I reckon," groaned Billy—the poor lad hadn't reached past the second row. He rolled a two, which got him nowhere. "So how's about your machine, Cecil?"

"What's that? You want to know how my machine's doing?" Cecil had grown extremely fond of the boy, but sometimes his regional brogue was hard to decipher, especially for a man who'd never even visited northern England.

"Yeah. I mean apart from t' missin' piece, have you figured it out yet? Why it brung us so far from 'ome. 'Ave you fixed it?"

"Bugg...darn it." Cecil's three landed him on the next snake head and sent him four rows down to Billy's level. "Oh, not yet. There's still something I can't quite get my head around."

"'Ave you told it to Garrett? 'E's a right good 'un wi' knowin' what to do in a tricky spot. I reckon there's no one like 'im." The lad's eyes glazed and he looked down, trying to blink the dampness away. Cecil's urge to take Billy in his arms and reassure him that he had nothing to worry about triggered a sore memory. His own son's tendency to cry when he'd been very young had led to the lad being picked on at school, and Cecil had raised hell with the headmaster when nothing had been done about the bullying. A sharp echo of that livid quarrel made him wince. Billy needed a father figure, someone to look up to. And he had chosen an excellent role model.

"Indeed. Lord Embrey's a rare fellow. I daresay he's the best of us in a tricky spot. But I'm afraid he hasn't solved our problem yet. Nor has Captain Champlain. It's something beyond our understanding...for the time being."

"My mam always said lookin' for t' simplest answer first were usually t' best way. She said my dad were always makin' things complicated when they weren't really." The boy's next throw landed him at the foot of a ladder, taking him up five rows.

"That's good advice. Your mother was wise."

"Yeah." Billy sniffled, then wiped his nose on his sleeve. His amusingly sheepish expression suggested he'd often been chided for not using a handkerchief. "My mam taught piano."

Taught—past tense. Cecil handed the lad his own handkerchief. "That notion of the simplest explanation

138

is a big one in science, Billy. It's often the most straightforward connection that…we miss…"

"Eh? What's the matter? Cecil? It's your go."

Straightforward connection…simplest explanation…

The boy tugged at his waistcoat and stared at him as though he wasn't sure Cecil was still breathing.

"Billy, can I ask you something important?"

"I reckon."

"It's about your book."

"Yeah? What about it?"

Let me get this straight in my mind. 1908…the storm…the ice cream vehicle on the embankment…

"Billy, what were you thinking about when the time jump occurred? At that *precise* moment when the storm vanished and sunlight appeared."

Retrieving his book from the deck behind him, Billy opened to a double-page illustration depicting several dinosaurs in their natural habitat. The coloured pencil sketch was well-drawn but the backdrop appeared somewhat tropical and idealized.

"It were this picture. I were frightened by all t' chasin', an' I went an' hid in my dad's coat. All them bright lights from t' factory made me think of that comet—you know, that big 'un that killed all t' dinosaurs off. That were t' last thing I thought about."

"The dinosaurs?"

"Yeah, I reckon."

Could that be the answer? As far-fetched as it sounded, it was frankly the *only* theory he'd come across even remotely linking 1908 with the Cretaceous Period. And with the advent of the perfect spider web in his factory, this metaphysical can of worms had already been flung open. But what actually, physically linked the two phenomena? Somehow, a boy's imaginings had veered the most advanced machine ever created millions of years off course?

How in the name of—

"So you think I were to blame for all this?" Billy's inscrutable stare bored deeper and deeper into Cecil's flimsy reasoning.

"Not at all, lad. Of course not." He could never let the boy think that. And this grave line of questioning had lasted long enough. "It's one of a hundred theories I've had that doesn't hold up. There's no scientific basis…any more than there is for why your sarsaparilla tastes better here in the time of the dinosaurs than it ever did back home."

"Yeah. I always liked that an' all. Garrett said it were good too. *I say.*" Billy's imitation of Embrey's posh accent was spot on. The deck rocked a little as Cecil laughed. Commotion among the crew at the stern lasted only a moment and then all went silent. A second shimmy sent Kibo dashing across the quarterdeck, and a faint splash in the distance drew telescopes from pockets. But no one appeared unduly alarmed.

"All right, here we go…" Cecil blew into his fist as he shook the die, "…no more snakes for me. From now on, I'm the snake *charmer.*" He rolled a five and climbed another ladder to dizzy heights.

Billy folded his arms and pouted. "See, I told yer it were bloody rigged."

Their bubbles columned into the bell's fading light. Verity tugged hard on her lifeline, signalling she was ready for Djimon to hoist her back up. Still no response. She'd already yanked the line over a dozen times to no avail. But now, with darkness smothering the lake bed, Embrey sensed things were getting desperate.

Where the hell are you, Djimon?

She lit another flare and he breathed easier. Though the bell hung a mere several fathoms above them, it might as well be a nautical mile because the weight of their deep sea diving suits anchored them to the bottom. He anticipated her next gesture—to cast off their weights and swim up—as quickly as he feared it. The pressure at this depth was considerable, and without helmets, they would have to exhale as they ascended slowly, to avoid gases building up in the bloodstream. If they didn't, a potential air embolism might prove fatal.

He shut his eyes and tried to remain calm.

Verity jabbed his shoulder to get his attention. Her harsh gaze yanked him back to immediate obedience. She mimed what she was about to do and then raised her eyebrows, as if to ask, do you understand?

Embrey gave an emphatic nod.

Oh, God, please let this work.

First, he clumsily unbuckled his heavy boots. Verity then sliced his ballast weights free with her knife. Finally, he took a deep breath and she unfastened and lifted his helmet. The flood of icy water seized his skull. She pointed up. He began kicking and clawing his way to the bell as though it was the last pocket of life anywhere in existence. He exhaled a few bubbles after every few strokes. The fog of spores and plankton made him think he was lost in a giant pea soup. Progress seemed glacial until he spied a not-quite-circular shape in the gloom. Lines dangled from it like distended veins. One last spurt brought him to within arm's reach. He gripped the rim and his momentum lifted him into the bell with surprising grace.

The first thing he noticed in the dim light was a dark stain on the metal floor. *God help us. Has Djimon—*

"Here! Take it!"

While coughing his guts up, he took the kaleidoscope from Verity and then helped her climb in and somehow wrapped her in a blanket. She wound the dynamo handle until all the lights blazed on. Shaking uncontrollably, she spied the pool of blood. The rim of the moon pool, too, had buckled. Something large and powerful had to have broken through, snatching poor Djimon.

She collapsed onto the floor and stared at the damaged brass rim.

"I'm sorry, Verity."

She brushed his hand away. They sat in stunned silence. The gentle echo-popping sounds of droplets on lapping water, the whir of the dynamo, and Verity's quiet sniffles conspired to deafen his thoughts. Finally he rose to his knees. "Okay, we did what we set out to do, so where do we go from here?"

"To hell, I hope."

"All right, but *then* where?"

"Remind me to kill that pompous bastard when we make it back." She thumped the copper wall.

"Who? Reardon?" No reply. "Granted, but how—"

"How the buggery did you *think* we were going to get back?" Verity's shout pierced his already aching ears. "For God's sake, get out of my way." She pushed him aside and snatched up what looked like a hollow telephone receiver on the end of a hose. She spoke into it, waited for a reply.

"And they'll haul us up?"

"Uh-huh." She rolled her eyes. "Shut up and don't speak to me again."

Embrey waited until her face was downturned and then flicked her a mocking salute. He drank a few cupped handfuls of fresh water from the moon pool. It tasted crisp, marvellous.

Then he recoiled, remembering what swam down there, and what might appear again at any moment...

Over twenty minutes later, with no reply from the *Empress,* Verity leapt up and turned her back to him. "Help me off with this thing."

Words he'd give anything to hear under any other circumstance.

"We're swimming the rest of the way?" he asked.

"No choice, I'm afraid."

The chilling finality hit him. Something *had* happened on the surface, and if it worried someone like Verity... "We could wait a bit longer, see if they—"

"No. We've waited long enough," she said.

"But what if it's just a problem with the communication cable? Say something bit through it. They'll hoist us up after a set time has elapsed without word, surely."

Verity's dripping hair appeared almost gunmetal brown in the dimming light. "Yes, and that time has elapsed." She wound the dynamo once more. "The auxiliary diver checks in every five minutes. After fifteen without contact, the deck crew automatically begins hoisting. Trust me, Embrey, we are on our own. Whatever happened to Djimon may have happened to the *Empress* as well. Now get this thing off me."

He obeyed, but the thought of finding an empty deck—he'd left Billy and Reardon up there, for Christ's sake—turned his stomach. Even the sight of Verity in her underwear served only to remind him of how vulnerable they were and how much he needed this ordeal to be over. He wasn't Garrett Embrey right now—he was simply another creature in the primordial soup, snatching at survival. Nothing else mattered.

She helped him out of his clingy suit and they both peered into the moon pool.

"Remember to exhale steadily all the way up." Her words were soft, distracted.

"I will."

"I'll take the clock part."

"No, the strongest swimmer should carry it."

Verity blinked at him, her pink-and-white face elfin and beautiful. "Embrey, I do this for a living."

"But I haven't done a damn thing to help on this dive. At least let me take this risk for you." He picked up the kaleidoscope and slid into the water, gauging her reaction.

Verity shook her head slowly.

He sighed, then handed her the clock part. "Can't blame me for trying."

"Crazy fool. You'd never have made it like that anyway." She cut a length of rope, tied one end to the gadget and the other to her ankle.

"Ah."

She gently splashed his face. "Don't look back, *omafimbo odula*. Whatever happens, kick until you taste home. I'll be with you all the way."

"Promise?"

After her quick nod, he took three deep breaths and submerged. He kicked away from the bell, confident that he could swim the breadth of an ocean if Verity were beside him. He climbed with a muscular stroke, never doubting, never looking back. The cream umbilical cable stretched forever upward. Lighter hues flickered above him like an emerald stampede on a glass ceiling.

He finally surfaced, gasping for his life on the starboard side of the *Empress*. Verity sprang up beside him, equally spent. But no one greeted them from the open hatches across the bulwark or through the porthole windows.

"Remember, we've surfaced far too quickly after such a long dive," she said. "It's dangerous. If you should start to feel sickly, use the oxygen canister or drink plenty of—Look! The bow!" She pointed him to a dent in the iron plane, then to several harpoons floating near the stern, still attached to their lines. "They've been attacked all right. *Ahoy! Kibo! Anyone aboard?*"

Embrey yelled with her but they received no response.

"Come on." She urged him to swim after her. "They may have abandoned ship."

"Yes, and it must have been for a good reason," he called after her, but she didn't stop. "Hey, wait for me."

As they climbed aboard, spilling streams as they crept, the empty ship groaned. She set the kaleidoscope down on the quarterdeck. Blood speckled the deck around two of the open starboard hatches and one of the port ones as well. One of the two lifeboats was also missing.

Embrey noticed a V shape floating off the starboard bow. It appeared heavy, as it didn't bob with the undulating lake. He glanced at the erect davits that had lifted the lifeboat over the side, then at the V shape again. "Please tell me that isn't what I think it is."

She gave a deep sigh. "I'm afraid so."

"How many would it have held?"

"All of them, Embrey. God help us, I think we've lost them *all*."

Chapter 13

Prehistoric Campfire

How a mission could at once be successful and yet fail so utterly tore Verity's thoughts in two as she wandered B-deck, trying to figure out the chain of events leading to this disaster. For one, the iron rig for the bell winch was bent, which explained why the crew hadn't been able to hoist them up. But *why* was it bent? Had the leviathan they'd faced on the lake bed become snagged in the umbilical somehow? Had that same monster attacked the *Empress* out of spite? Perhaps it had the ability to leap out of the water, as high as the ship's deck. With the dinosaur's sixty-foot length, that wasn't much of a stretch.

Broken rifles and smashed harpoon launchers described a desperate last stand. The bulwark was damaged around virtually every open hatch, so the leviathan had to have attacked repeatedly on all sides. And poor little Billy. What a horrible nightmare for such a young boy. She should have insisted he and Reardon stay on A-deck with Tangeni.

A bitter welling in her throat made her swallow hard several times but it was no use.

This was her fault, *her* unforgivable blunder.

Without Reardon, it's all been for nothing.

She ran to the nearest open hatch and threw up over the side.

"How long before Tangeni returns?" Embrey asked.

"Until we signal. He'll keep circling until we signal."

"I don't see him."

Verity spat the noxious taste from her mouth and wiped her lips. "You will. But it's all for nothing now." They would have to survive here until they died, in this prehistoric nether-world, with no hope of seeing home ever again.

"Nothing we could have done, Verity. It was only a matter of time." His glistening Adonis physique seemed alien, a mirage. Seeing his full collar-to-hip scar for the first time made her feel a little sorry for him—he'd been through so much and had worked tirelessly to protect the others, and for what? "I daresay fate was set against us the minute we arrived," he said. "It was a forlorn hope after all."

"And a cruel twist. It didn't have to end like this. We could have—"

"*Garrett!* You made it!"

They both spun toward the engine room at the stern. Men in blue uniform filed out, elated and self-congratulatory, as though part of some obscene April Fool's prank. It took a moment for Verity to register the change of events. If these crewmen had been here all along, why hadn't they answered her calls? But then—she hadn't called since climbing aboard...

"Garrett!" Young Billy sprinted for his half-naked guardian, and Embrey flung his arms around the boy and lifted him high. Still she couldn't quite take it in. Had the undersea pressure affected her more than she realised? Yet, seeing Professor Reardon appear at the engine room door, his shirt sleeves rolled up and bloody, plucked her heart and made it thrum.

Their dive had *not* been for nought. Djimon's sacrifice had lasting worth, and she need despair no more. Even Kibo emerged from his engine room, still impeccably dressed, striding like a victorious gambler.

"*Eembu,* I knew you'd make it." He shook her hand. His impressive grin made her puff and exhale with nervous relief. The habit of command dictated she retain a measure of composure at all times, but damn it if she couldn't cry out with joy. Another crewman—Kwame— draped a windproof jacket over her.

"Thank you, thank you." She cleared her throat, oddly embarrassed by all the attention. "Embrey and I achieved our goal, but," and her high jinks sank, "we lost Djimon, I'm afraid."

Kibo winced and looked away to the sunken lifeboat. "Then his spirit joins another three of our number, and Mr. Briory was killed, as well."

"No. What happened?"

"Let us reach shore first, then I will describe our ordeal. Stay clear of the sides, you men." He scolded two of his engine crew, then led Verity to the buckled bell winch. "I think we should cut the bell loose, *Eembu.* There is no way to hoist it up, and the only reason I didn't cast if free and head back to shore is because you were still down there."

Verity gently squeezed his arm. "You did well, my friend. Grace under pressure, that's what I like to see."

"I am sorry Djimon won't be with us. The whole crew liked his…affableness—is that the correct word?"

She smiled. "Close enough, brother. That's close enough. Now go ahead, get us underway. Have Kwame and MacDonald cut the bell hose."

"Aye, Captain."

Meanwhile, Reardon wrapped the brass clockwork in his waistcoat and hurried it back to the safety of the engine room, pausing only to compliment Verity on her "brave show, which may have saved all our necks."

"You're welcome, Profess—" But he was already out of earshot, deep in consternation. After all, there was no guarantee the intricate part hadn't been damaged beyond repair.

Billy tugged her jacket down until she matched his height, and then hugged her for the longest time. Such a sweet, affectionate boy—he reached for Embrey's hand and pulled him down to share the embrace. An extraordinary pang of contentment, fleeting though it was, made her feel…complete somehow. Alive and unguarded. Embrey's hand nestled on the back of her neck, and her heart began to *thump, thump, thump*…

"You jus' described that exact same 'un what attacked us." Billy flicked to the appropriate page in his dinosaur book. "Lio-pleu-ro-don—that's how Cecil says it. Big paddle-like limbs and massive, strong jaws like a crocodile, only it were a lot bigger than what it says in 'ere."

"We estimated between fifty and sixty feet, didn't we?" Verity turned to Embrey. He wasn't really listening, and instead watched with fascination the re-coupling of A and B decks. Tangeni had begun his descent, and as B-deck was now moored on the lake shore, this promised to be a routine attachment. Verity's men had already raised the guide spars to catch A-deck's descending hull. The airship's link chains dangled ready to be caught and locked into position. Her only concern was that the liopleurodon attacks had bent the bulwarks out of shape—a misalignment of the two decks meant they could not be cranked back into place together. The *Empress Matilda* might be divorced for good.

"Whose idea was the lifeboat, Billy?" She'd already heard the tale from Kibo but wanted to keep the youngster's attention. The re-coupling was a deafening procedure—iron clanking and scraping on iron—and to a child, the sudden claustrophobic weight that bore down upon B-deck might be a frightening experience.

"Um, it were Cecil's idea." The lad blankly poured over the pages of his book. "After two men were snatched, 'e reckoned we had to do somethin' quick. That bloody lio-pleu-ro-don kept jumpin' out of the water, bashin' against the side of the ship. 'E smashed us underwater an' nearly capsized us. That's when it got them first 'uns—them two aeronauts—they slid to the hatches and the monster got 'em." He glanced up at Verity, then gripped the bell house rail next to Embrey as B-deck's hull darkened the sky. "So Cecil said we should rig a lifeboat with some hydrogen canisters an' let the monster attack it. Hydrogen explodes, see. 'E wanted the other men to shoot the canisters while the dinosaur were attackin' that lifeboat." Billy's storytelling grew nervous and rapid. "But it were over with too quick an' nobody got a shot off before the boat were sunk. Next time we were tipped on our side, Briory rolled into the bugger's jaws an' we never saw 'im again."

Clank, clank went the airship's hull onto the guide spars as Verity's men rushed about fastening the link chains into place. B-deck scraped into position simply enough, and the *Empress* groaned as she leaned to one side under the extra weight.

Embrey gave her an appreciative nod, as if he hadn't been convinced the re-coupling could work, before joining the aft capstan team to crank the decks together once and for all.

She sent Billy to Reardon in the engine room, out of harm's way, and then rotated the forward capstan with her last remaining crewmen. The final *clank* of a Gannet's re-coupling usually heralded several hearty huzzahs. This time, dead silence.

She sighed as the whole ship lifted from the beach. Gallons of purged ballast thundered from A-deck into the kelpy shallows. She'd lost many good men these past few days—far too many. At this rate, would *anyone* be left alive to make the time jump?

Snuggled alone in the bough nest, a single blanket cushioning his backside from the cold metal floor, Embrey wrapped his arms around his knees and took in the spectacular prehistoric sunset. At this soundless height, where only creaks from the balloon canopies kept him company, the vastness of this unvisited world stretched eerily in every direction. Neither car horns nor clattering hooves nor the bark of a feral dog emerged from London's streets as he watched. He was truly some place he should not be.

Before mankind would rise to prominence, the entire known lifespan of Mount Everest had to unfold. According to Reardon, the number of days from here to 1908 was comparable to the number of stars in a small galaxy. And unless the machine worked, they would all die before the first rose ever spread its petals. This was so long ago, even romance didn't exist.

The police chase through the storm seemed an epoch ago. Hell, Reardon's accidental intervention had occurred in the nick of time...the *literal* nick of time. Unspeakable, yes, but fortuitous all the same. Given the choice between being hanged for treason or lost in a forgotten world, he was perhaps the only one, apart from Reardon, who'd secretly thanked his lucky stars for this accident.

"Ahoy, night owl." A woman's voice made him jump.

"Who goes there?"

Verity poked her head up over the rail. "First the depths, now the clouds? We really need to keep our feet on the ground, Embrey."

"What are you doing up here?"

"What are you?" She climbed into the nest and crouched opposite him—to bring bad news? Berate him for coming up here without her permission?

"For some peace and quiet," he said. "I fancied soaking up a little prehistoric magic—you know, before the back-breaking begins. This looked as good a spot as any."

"I never pegged you for a deep-thinking fellow, Embrey."

Seeing her dressed once more in her safari outfit— blouse, flared jodhpurs, half chaps and boots— quickened his pulse and recalled the time he'd seen her climbing the steps outside her cabin, in those last promise-filled moments before she'd turned on him. But that feud had been her doing, her prejudice. He'd done nothing except bear an innocent family name.

153

"You look worried," she said. "Did I say something wrong?"

"Not exactly—well, not recently—"

She sighed, blinking her big, inscrutable hazel eyes. Embrey loved the way her lace cuffs, too big for her wrists, flapped in the breeze. But there wasn't even the hint of an apology forthcoming. Not good enough.

"Things were said that can't easily be forgotten. First you humiliated me in front of the entire congregation, then you insulted Father—without even bothering to hear my story."

She narrowed her eyes. "You ass! I came up here in—"

"If you'll let me finish—*for Christ's sake*—I simply meant to say, I would like a chance to finally explain myself. You've heard one side of the story, the poisoned version, and yet you carry on half-cocked and continually ridicule me in public. I'll not stand for it a moment longer."

She lifted her eyebrows. "Oh, and I suppose my half-cocked rescue when you fell over the side counts for nothing? Those insults—they may have been hasty."

"Are you saying you no longer hold my family responsible?"

"I wouldn't go that far."

"Then allow me to speak my piece. You need to be enlightened."

"Ha! Please, by all means, *enlighten* me, Your Worship." Her snootiness knew no bounds, but if he were in her position, he might very well react with the same scepticism.

"Very well," he said. "You suffered a terrible loss in Benguela. And you understandably accepted the official story of my father's collusion in the rebel attack. Not a single newspaper anywhere in the empire, to my knowledge, printed a dissenting article." He paused to catch his breath. "But when you've known a man as closely and for as long as I knew my father, when his unblemished military record and love for the empire are unquestioned by everyone who knew him well, when Britannia's prosecuting arm is twisted behind her back by a notoriously corrupt body like the Leviacrum Council, when evidence is demonstrably falsified and then whisked from further public scrutiny to ensure a quick execution, you can understand why I no longer have any love for the empire."

"With all due respect, every family of a convicted man cries foul. Why should I take your word over that of the Council?"

"What rock have you been hiding under? Good Lord, woman." Before she could retort, he gave a loud sigh. "Verity, you must have heard the rumours."

"No." The lines in her puzzled frown might as well have said, Made by the Corps. "Pray tell. I haven't lived in London for years."

"Well, the Leviacrum towers serve no practical purpose, do they? Thousands of feet tall and for what?"

"Why build anything ambitious?" She shrugged. "It needn't imply a sinister motive."

"Verity, you can't afford to be this naive. If we return to 1908—"

"*When* we return."

"—the Leviacrum Council is going to arrest Reardon and execute me for treason against the Crown. Don't you see? The Council *is* the Crown, the government, the empire. British subjects everywhere are unwittingly pledging their allegiance to a secret society turned dictatorial power. They have subverted our democracy through science—steam technology has revolutionized the empire, and most of the patents for those inventions have been bought or bribed from private citizens. Over eighty percent of the nation's wealth is subordinate to the Council, in one way or another. Trust me when I say the Freemasons are tadpoles compared to the bigwigs controlling the Leviacra."

He raked his hair behind his ears. "Shortly after my father returned from Angola, he was approached several times to join something called the Atlas Club, and the offers kept him up nights. I never did find out why, or what the club itself actually was. But when he refused for the umpteenth time, explaining he was already a member of too many clubs and societies…he suddenly found himself facing an indictment for treason. It was odd, though, I didn't connect the two events until much later. But here's the clincher—my Uncle Ralph was *also* approached about the Atlas Club in the run-up to *his* arrest. He'd turned it down, as well."

He paused while a chorus of distant roars from the coast suggested large dinosaurs were engaged in vicious combat.

"This is all very…conspiratorial, Embrey. You'd have us believe the devil resides in that copper tower, and his minions stand watch at every street corner. I say, show a fool his shadow and he'll show you a shady world."

"And if it really *is* a corrupt world?"

Verity laughed. "Then the joke is on me. But I'd like to hear more about your father's trial. You say evidence was falsified. Have you proof of this?"

"No. Like I said, the evidence disappeared after the trial. The two handwriting experts they used were never heard from again."

"As you say—very odd."

Despite her obtuse remarks, Embrey felt sure he'd made his case, and that was enough for now. They were on cordial speaking terms. No need to overstep his good fortune. And surely he could think of something more congenial than politics to engage a beautiful woman during a sunset.

"I wonder, Verity, if we'd met somewhere else—" he began carefully, "—on safari in Africa, say, or in South America…"

His mind blanked.

"Hmm?" She appeared to blink coquettishly without realising, which made his heart squirrel.

"I only meant to say that, a few years back, if we'd shot each other on safari—*met*—I mean *met* each other on safari…" *Kill me now!* "…I'd have asked permission to call on you."

She stared at him. Embrey wondered how long it would take his body to hit the deck if he jumped to save his further humiliation. But…was she…blushing?

"Would I have been too bold?" he asked.

"That depends."

"On what?"

She smirked. "On where our bullets had hit."

Chapter 14

Cecil's Diary

My dearest Edmond,

A happy turn of events! Today, Miss Polperro and her Whitehall comrades agreed to help us collect timber from the western forest. Only three days have passed since our adventure on the great lake and already our two factions appear to have coalesced. No more bickering, at least. Embrey doesn't entirely trust this truce—he says he'd rather work cheek by jowl with a pig than a politician—but I'm relieved to have an end to the animosity. And with Carswell's discovery of a freshwater brook in that same woods, our makeshift industry is running very well indeed. Kibo's constant conveyance of timber and water on his tri-wheel vehicle is a godsend. I estimate in three days' time we should have enough materials to power my machine. That ought to be more than sufficient.

When you are old enough to understand the physics of my invention, I shall explain how difficult it has been to realign the lenses for refracting psammeticum energy, and also why I believe young Billy's imagination—his conscious thought at the instant of the time jump—determined our destination. My Harrison clock must somehow, during the reaction, have tapped into the very "consciousness" of time itself. Not in any human or even God-like sense, that age-old, perhaps infinite dimension we call time must be some sort of medium of exchange. It is not merely a cold abstract. It has a direct, determinable link to every molecule and every minute flow of energy ever found in the universe. We can interface with it, inject our thoughts and memories into it, and it will accordingly effect a time shift around our localised reaction. Is cosmic psammeticum energy itself a part of the physical memory of the universe?

Among all the thoughts conjured by our learned minds during the time jump, those of a young boy determined our destination. This, to me, suggests a child's imagination is the purer form of consciousness. It is uncluttered by adult ambivalence and ambiguity. And the spider's web? Well, what could be purer than animal instinct? This great force we have tapped into seems to react strongest to the simplest motivations of the living brain. One of escape—Billy's; and the economy of survival—the spider's perfect web.

Those are my theories, at least. In a few days time, I shall put them to the test and have Billy conjure a vivid memory of London. Aught else and I fear Miss Polperro's objection—that resting our entire endeavour on a child's capricious mind is a folly—may well be proven correct. But there is no alternative. We cannot leave him behind, and we must therefore have faith in his powers of concentration.

Lord knows, I wish it were not so. In all other capacities, I feel confident my machine will perform wonders once again. And this diary may yet find its way into your adult hands, my dear son. I have given everything to see you again. Let God stop us if He must.

A reclining moon hung low over the southern tree tops as Cecil drank a toast with his fellow dinner guests to the London they'd left behind and the one they would soon be reacquainted with. The officers' dining table had been brought up to the quarterdeck for this unusual get-together—for the first time, Agnes Polperro had deigned to attend a discussion on the upcoming time travel, specifically to voice her comrades' opinions. She sat opposite Verity and the two said little throughout the meal, while Cecil, Embrey and Tangeni regaled each other with tales of the lake expedition.

At last, as Embrey poured the after-dinner wine, the prissy schoolmarm folded up her napkin and flicked it rudely onto the table. "Let us not play out this charade any longer. We are here to discuss the boy—a boy whose very presence puts our chances of returning home, indeed our lives, in jeopardy. Your views on the matter, Professor Reardon, are reckless and dangerous as ever, but I would like to hear what the rest of you have to say. Bear in mind you are playing with not only your own lives and the lives of this crew, but also those of fourteen gentlemen of some note in London, and my own future, as well. Do not be swayed by sentiment alone. Think carefully on the wisdom of trusting our fate to a fickle boy. Most of my colleagues are ambivalent as to whether he should be allowed to come with us at all."

Incredible! Cecil had heard the rumours but this—actually *considering* leaving Billy behind? An eleven-year-old lad?

"Not while I draw breath, you don't." He leapt up in protest and slammed his fist on the table.

Embrey joined him, hands on hips...or was it pistols? "I think the matter is already settled, ma'am." How he kept such a calm voice eluded Cecil, but clearly young Embrey was used to confrontations of all types. "Anyone who doesn't wish to make the journey alongside the boy is welcome to remain here. That is every man's prerogative...and every woman's." He eyed Miss Polperro harshly. "Is anyone else here seriously considering this madness? Tangeni? Verity?"

"Absolutely not." The African pursed his lips.

"Verity?" Embrey appeared as puzzled by her silence as Cecil was. Surely she wasn't—

"*Eembu,* what are you thinking?" Even Tangeni was at a loss.

The captain took a long swig of wine, her attractive elfin features lit severely by the oil lamp. "I'd like to hear Miss Polperro's proposal first. That was not an easy thing for her to say, or for her colleagues to agree on. If those learned men have a solution, I'd like to hear it."

"Sincerely?" Cecil couldn't believe his ears. "In all my years, I've never heard such a heinous—"

"Sit down, Professor," Verity insisted with her forefinger pointed at his seat. "We've listened to your opinions ad nausea this past week, and if it's all the same with you, I'd like to hear what our Whitehall friends have to say."

"No, that is not all right, and never will be. Good night, Embrey, Tangeni."

But before he could leave the table, Verity shot to her feet. "I said sit down. Right this instant!"

How dare she? Cecil's narrowest glare didn't appear to have even the slightest effect. *Doesn't she realise this is* my *show and no one else's?*

161

He threw his own napkin down and reluctantly obeyed...this time. She was, after all, in charge of his protection. He'd need her on his side while he completed the repairs to his machine.

"And you too, Embrey, if you wouldn't mind," she said.

The young marquess bowed and took his seat—surprising, given they'd been at loggerheads for much of the week.

"Pray explain, then, Miss Polperro." Cecil cast her an icy glare. "What do you propose we do with our errant schoolboy?"

"Nothing. You all misapprehend my objections, as usual. And this is precisely why a military officer with no actual command experience should never have put herself in charge of the camp." *Yes, and your bustle makes you like look like a march hare.* "While I respect your diplomacy just now, Lieutenant Champlain, you were not voted to your current position. On the other hand, there are several experienced members of Parliament whose counsel you have utterly ignored. Granting us governorship over those crumbling buildings was an insult. Your divisive attempt at leadership has brought ruin to this camp."

Verity raised an eyebrow and then pinged her glass with a fork. "So says the head of a lynch mob, speaking on behalf of—"

"But they were drunk at the time, drowning their sorrows. It is not fair to...after all, they were only riled by the truth." And so was Miss Polperro, her voice now sharp and strict. "I cannot excuse their behaviour, but nor do I have to."

"Then kindly refrain from casting aspersions on Miss Champlain's conduct," Embrey replied, to everyone's delight—everyone who didn't resemble a put-upon schoolmarm at parents' evening, that was.

"Answer me this one thing." Verity stared down her Whitehall counterpart. "What would you have us do with Billy?"

"Leave him behind with some of the aeronauts. Let us first make the time jump without his caprice, and then let Professor Reardon return for him later, when fewer lives are at stake. The Leviacrum Council would spare no resource in finding a solution to these phenomena with Professor Reardon. I will pledge my career to helping you return for Billy, but first let us save as many lives as we can…with as low a risk as possible. In my view, that is the only responsible way to proceed."

"And what if I am never able to pinpoint this exact date? It might take a thousand time jumps to find him." Cecil's lip began to tremble.

Tangeni tapped his palm on the tabletop. "Also, the time jump might not happen the same way without Billy. Surely we should have things as they were the first time, or as close as we can possibly get them."

"All relevant arguments." Adjusting her shawl over her shoulders, Miss Polperro rose daintily. "But I believe I have stated my case well enough. My objection stands. However you choose to proceed, I pray it is for the good of the camp, and not mere sentiment alone. We await your informed decision. Good night, gentlemen, Lieutenant Champlain."

A single oil lamp burned for her on the embankment. They waited a few minutes until it disappeared with her up Bridge Street, then they continued their discussion.

Embrey piped up first. "I say, does anyone else have that smarting sensation, like they've just served detention? My knuckles feel thoroughly rapped."

"Oh, she's a piece of work alright," Verity said. "And dangerous. I wouldn't want her within ten eons of my children, if I ever have any. But at least we know what's been bubbling in her cauldron all this while."

"I've never heard anything so cold and calculating." Tangeni belched and, after a silent rebuke from his captain, quickly apologized.

"To state the obvious, then, we're not considering Whitehall's proposal, even for a second?" The thought of Billy being snatched in the middle of the night by cowardly politicians made Cecil's chest flame. What lethal action *wouldn't* he take if that ever happened? None. He'd murder anyone by any means necessary to prevent them from abducting Edmond...*Billy* from him. *I swear to God, I will.*

"That goes without saying, Professor. And I'd like to apologize for being short with you earlier. It was for her sake," Verity said. "I wanted her to think I was open to any reasonable solution. It was the only way to get her to speak honestly. If we'd all shot her proposal down *before* she'd proposed it, I fear we'd now be hypothesizing rather than lamenting. She has shown her true colours— they all have. We are now fully primed."

"Bravo, Verity!" Embrey raised his glass and flicked her a mischievous grin.

"And with that, I will bid you good night, gentlemen." She yawned and left for her cabin before the men had a chance to stand up.

164

When she'd closed her door behind her, Embrey leaned over the table and whispered, "Let's we three make a pact, then. Tangeni? Reardon? Let us promise to never leave Billy unguarded until all this is over. Verity has enough on her plate overseeing the camp. So whatever happens, at least one of *us* must stay with him at all times. Agreed?"

"I'm with you, Embrey." Tangeni shook his hand. "Whatever happens, you have my word."

The mellifluous amber light intensified both men's gazes. Where a minute ago Cecil's protective urge had been private, contained, it now blazed out into the night air with shared fierceness. Two of the best men he'd ever known were watching over Billy with him. A relieved tear slid down his trembling cheek.

Rather than wipe it away, he extended both hands to his friends across the table. "Thank you," he said. "Thank you both. Whatever happens, I will never forget it."

Chapter 15

Following Quatermain

At noon on the day before their scheduled departure through time, Verity and Embrey headed a hunting party to the western forest. A plague of black, weevil-like organisms infested much of the *Empress's* food reserves, and Polperro's posse had all but run out of their meagre rations. While in her own time it was common enough for sailors and aeronauts to eat weevil-ridden meals, here in prehistory the grubs were an unknown entity. They might be poisonous, perhaps lethal. She therefore had little choice but to buttress these final days' supplies— and maybe several others besides, if Reardon's machine couldn't find 1908—with as much dinosaur meat as Kibo's car could carry.

Her engine man stopped the tri-wheel vehicle and ice cream trailer at the tree-line ahead of them and waited. The long grass fell away to a damp, spongy moss for the last hundred yards to the forest. Embrey's over-the-ankle boots with white, spat-style uppers appeared ridiculous for any kind of wild terrain, but he was just as sure-footed as Verity. He also looked strikingly handsome in his winged-collared shirt and decorative waistcoat. Behind him, Carswell and his two cronies kept to themselves, while Reba, Philomena and three more of her crew continuously scanned the trees on all sides.

"What's the biggest thing you've hunted, Embrey?" *Let him brag.* A little macho hubris might go a long way to making her feel she was in familiar company. During her years spent with African hunters-turned-aeronauts, she had grown fond of that peculiar male tendency to extol one's own life-or-death conquests as a measure of one's masculinity. It was dumb, yes, but also, on occasion, reassuring.

"Why?" he replied.

"You don't think it pertinent, considering our goal?"

He shrugged and loosened his collar. "Not especially. I'm by far the best shot here. Is that good enough for you?"

It was.

"What's eating you, Verity...so to speak? You've faced leviathans of the deep and not flinched. A little hunting wouldn't bring this on. What's the matter?"

Was her anxiety so clear on her face? How well he knew her and yet how little. To think she hadn't been stricken with absolute fear when they'd faced the liopleurodon gave her more credit than she deserved. But on this he was right; an unspoken fear had nagged at her ever since their tryst in the bough nest. Its insidious, gnawing quality was affecting both her appetite and her sleep. With all the incredible goings-on around her, that one personal question should preoccupy her mind like this was not something a captain should admit.

And yet, if she didn't ask now, time was running out...

"Embrey?"

"Yes."

"You're wanted for treason. What are you going to do when we return to London?"

He halted, shrugged again and then carried on walking. "Whatever it is, it'll be on my own. I might be a wanted man, but I have means of…I know what to do."

Her insides turned queasy. What didn't he want her to know? Did he already have an escape plan? If so, would that be the last time she'd ever see him?

"Everyone check your weapons!" he shouted to the party. "Let's avoid any slip-ups *before* they happen. And no one goes anywhere alone." Then he said quietly to Verity, "I think we should pair Kibo with one of the Whitehall cronies, so he can spy on them."

"Agreed."

He looked away and briefly mimed a whistle. "And you and I…let's not separate."

Funny, I was thinking the same thing.

They trekked a good half hour past the trees they'd felled, into the heart of the forest, without spotting a single dinosaur of any notable size. Several skittish bipeds no bigger than house cats darted across their path, while Reba found a nest of large, broken eggs. Embrey said he'd tracked game through the Amazon jungle before, and the route they were following— already somewhat hewn and trampled—had been forged by an animal of stupendous size. He pointed out huge prints in the mud and pine needles, and whole branches plucked bare high up.

"Some kind of sauropod?" Verity recalled the general name for the largest long-necked dinosaurs described in Billy's book.

"A herd of them." Kibo pointed his rifle higher each time they stopped.

Distant roars kept everyone alert, and the constant threat of meeting a baryonyx ensured the group remained silent and tight-knit. Occasionally a quick-moving shadow passed over the forest and Verity squeezed the slippery stock and barrel of her weapon.

She remembered Mr. Briory when they happened upon an area populated by beautiful yellow flowers. One or two bees quested through them, and she affectionately named the flowers "Briories."

Shortly after, Embrey shot a lumbering, armour-plated quadruped through its upturned mouth, killing it. Philomena chased its even bigger cousin—about the size of a cow—into a glade and spent several bullets bringing it down.

No sooner had everyone rushed to congratulate her when she started back toward them, a look of terror frozen on her face. She began to shake uncontrollably.

"What is it?" Kibo caught her as she flopped in his arms, her eyes bulging like boiled eggs.

She mumbled something unintelligible over and over again before her partner, Reba, slapped her hard. "This no way for aeronaut to behave! Tell what you see."

"I…I see…" Everyone leaned in. "Look out. *Look out through the trees.*" The poor woman squirmed loose in a panic and then started to dance in the middle of the glade—a violent tribal dance reminiscent of one Verity had seen performed in Kenya when the first British airships had arrived to recruit African crews. It was as though she was warding off evil spirits.

"What's got her so spooked?" Despite being limp with trepidation—Philomena had *never* displayed fear like

169

this before—Verity cocked her rifle and ventured out toward the fallen dinosaur. Embrey followed close by.

Look through the trees?

She stood on the spot Philomena had reached and gazed northward. A brilliant glare, like the sun reflecting off the ribs of a rain-minted airship, blinded her. She rubbed her eyes and looked again. The glare spread lower, and she made out the infinite glimmers of sunlight on the ocean. They'd almost reached the coast.

A cloud passed over, removing the glare and revealing...

What?

She rubbed the daydream out of her eyes and gazed once more. The impossible only came into greater focus. Waves broke upon it. Pterosaurs perched on its broken tip. And wait...*there*...much farther away, like a chalk shape in the blue ether, *another*. How was this possible?

She whispered, "Pinch me, Embrey. This can't be real."

He didn't respond. He, too, was lost between worlds. For no other sight could have struck with such awe or such portentousness.

The farthest reached the clouds. The nearest was rusted and decrepit; it had crumbled and broken in two, its collapsed section lying half out of the water, touching the shore. In her own time, wars had been fought over them.

They were Leviacrum towers, and they had been put here long ago.

Chapter 16

Orphans of the Storm

By the time they'd dragged the carcasses to Kibo's vehicle and were making back for camp, the temperature plummeted. Heavy grey clouds blanketed the sky. Embrey had suffered enough British winters to recognise the clouds were laden with snow. Sure enough, before the party reached London, a blizzard swept over the field.

Every remaining man and woman helped hoist the carcasses onto the *Empress,* while news of the shocking discovery on the lake spread quicker than snow covering the dry deck. Embrey was only vaguely responsive to questions and events around him. A periodic lucidity jabbed at him, reminded him to put on a warm jacket, now see to Billy, now get up, now obey Verity's summons to her cabin.

He didn't appear to be the only one afflicted by this fractured state of mind either, as both Kibo and Reardon succumbed to long bouts of silence while the women talked. Verity's cabin seemed as alien to him as everything else in this limbo between past and present. At least Billy was safe on B-deck with Tangeni watching over him.

"And it was how old, if you had to guess?" Miss Polperro leaned forward on her elbow, enthused by the discovery.

Verity stopped biting her nails long enough to swig another mouthful of her brandy. "Ancient—the metalwork had mostly rusted away. I'd guess at hundreds, maybe thousands of years old. And the height of the thing, if it was still erect, would be far taller than the London Leviacrum we know. Maybe twice as tall." She paused, glancing at each of her guests in turn. "What do you suppose it all means, gentlemen? *When are we?*"

"Professor Reardon? Do you have a theory, sir?" Agnes Polperro hadn't addressed anyone so politely since Embrey had met her. She rested her chin on her fist, and gave the professor her full attention. What about this revelation had perked her spirits so?

Reardon sat up as if from a daze, cleared his throat and then swabbed the spittle from his chin with a handkerchief. "I'm sorry. Did you address me?"

"She was wondering if you'd solved the riddle, old boy," Embrey now spoke for the first time, himself wanting, *needing* some thread of logic with which to untangle the knot in his brain. "If not the Cretaceous, when the deuce are we?"

"Of course we're in the Cretaceous, always have been." The professor, suddenly animated, gesticulated with his hands as though he'd supped a full pot of coffee. "Briory's observations of the plant life proved that, as well as the geology. If you are all suspecting this is the distant future, and that dinosaurs have been reintroduced at some point—perhaps as some kind of time travelling zoo—think again. There is no evidence here of a former civilisation, apart from the old Leviacrum towers."

"Actually," Verity interrupted, "Embrey and I discovered a metal panel on the lake bed, miles away from the collapsed towers."

"A current could have moved it that distance, or a storm," Embrey replied.

"True enough." She resumed her nail-biting.

Elbows on his chair arms, Reardon formed a pensive V-shape with his forearms and touching fingertips under his chin. "No, my theory has the more straightforward logic, but its ramifications may be very disturbing indeed. It is obvious that sometime in the future—our future from a twentieth century perspective—the Leviacrum Council will harness time travel on a massive scale. Entire towers will be sent back through time. For what purpose I don't know. Perhaps giant mineral deposits were found in the past, almighty quantities of gold, or even diamond geodes begging to be mined. Maybe we have happened upon the ruins of this cross-temporal industry.

"But for whatever reason, it did not endure. They may have exhausted the resources, or this epoch red in tooth and claw got the better of them. The point is that they scarred prehistory in a major way, and in doing so changed it irrevocably." He shook his head, a grim smile of disbelief quivering his rectangular chin. "Think on it—by leaping back to precede all mankind had achieved, they altered it. Civilisation as we know it in the twentieth century, everything from ice cream cones to advanced steam technology, might not have come to pass but for that meddling millions of years before. Perhaps the influences were subtle, like the thriving of a species of crustacean on the Leviacrum's warm exterior around the boilers. Before the tower appeared in prehistory, that species was doomed to extinction. But now it becomes hardier and spreads, supplanting other species and changing the ecological system forever. The knock-on effect of that influence over millions of years might become the difference between sperm whales existing and not existing. Ponder the import of that result for man and marine life. The world is not the same place.

"My friends, we are living proof of history revised. All that we are may not be all we were meant to be."

"Or perhaps this was all *meant* to be," Miss Polperro argued. "What if the Maker resews fate around those frays, and ensures things return to His initial plan for us? We make these changes by travelling through time, but the Lord unmakes them in equally subtle ways. Nature's forces are all about balance. Maybe time has an underlying, reshaping force as well—the way a mountain rises and falls by the same subterranean forces. Over time, what is done is also undone. What we do here may ultimately have no more effect on 1908 than a fistful of salt thrown into the sea. Time and the sea will have dissolved the change, the addition. It only seems far-reaching to us because we perceive ourselves as the centre of the universe, when in fact we're inconsequential in the grand scheme. Nature is patient and resourceful, like the meandering river. She will resume her intended course because God's design is not so fickle as ours."

"Yes, but over millions of years, we're not a fistful of salt, we're a bloody great landslide!" Reardon wagged his finger at her, and Embrey felt himself ebbing and flowing on the convictions of these two learned scientists. "Nature isn't going to simply erase the legacy of those Leviacrum towers merely because they erode and eventually disappear. I tell you they have changed the face of the planet, and we are their progeny. Orphans, that's what we are—orphans of a temporal storm that's been raging for millions of years. And we knew nothing about it…until now."

Embrey's mind clicked into gear. "What about the other anomalies—the perfect web and Billy's influence on time travel? Could *they* have been caused by all this meddling with time? Has all this tampering with history damaged the very underlying forces Miss Polperro predicts? And time is simply springing leaks?"

They all pondered that for a while, until Kibo, who hadn't yet said a word, cleared his throat. "Professors, that is all fascinating, but can you please answer me this? If we return to 1908, will it be the same as when we left?"

Miss Polperro sat up. "Yes, I am certain of it. By whatever means, I believe those elements of time and fate will reconvene for us. You'll see."

"I wish I knew, friend." Reardon glanced at Kibo, then looked gravely at the carpet. "I wish I knew."

It was a hard truth to take, but even Reardon had had to concede that, when it came to time, they were all at sea.

Sunrise on the last day crept up on Verity as she lay wide awake in her bed, planning, hoping, dreading. In her years as a Gannet officer she'd grown accustomed to the wind's caprice, to the sea's insidious nature. But she'd always had precedent and knowledge to bear her out, mankind's millennia of experience lending her vital

175

intuition. Here, Reardon had baited a new, unquantifiable beast. He knew as little about time travel as the first *homo sapiens* who jumped off a cliff, copying the birds, did about flying. And she was along for the next leap!

Freezing fog and a dank half-light stilled the deck while she wandered out for a stroll. Sleet and rain had washed the snow away overnight. A vague smell of cooked meat, quite pleasant, still clung to the *Empress*. Though she'd insisted the unused parts of the dinosaur carcasses be buried to remove the scent of blood from the air, predators often had extraordinary senses of smell. Billy's book concurred. Dinosaurs could probably sniff out a feast miles away. Which way had the winds blown during the night?

Embrey waved to her from the poop deck. He wore an oversized blue slicker and a sou'wester. They were wet. How long had he been standing there?

"Odd, is it not?" He pointed to the vague shape of Big Ben. The hands on its clock face were barely visible. *Five past eight.* "How time has stopped *and* carried on? What do you suppose the world made of our disappearance? A great chunk of Westminster obliterated, leaving no evidence."

"The night-lights will be burning in the Leviacrum for quite some time, I imagine."

Embrey *hmmed,* turned to her. "May I ask you something?"

"Uh-huh." She pinched the ends of the blanket together under her chin.

"Am I all right in your book?"

"Excuse me?" To frown dutifully or give nothing away and inhale his sweet, unexpected surrender—she lost her bearings for a moment. "What do you mean?"

"I mean…is there a chance…could you possibly conceive of…with all that we… Oh, Good Lord, spit it out, Garrett!" He gave a deep, self-berating growl. "What I mean to say is, do you still hold me in contempt?"

No outward smile, but her satisfaction lightened her inside like a fresh ballonet. Then of a sudden it fell, and she recalled Bernie's graveside funeral—the blacks and greys billowing austerely, the droning preacher reciting secondhand testimonies from friends and family, the passing of simple joy from her young world. It seemed only yesterday. So much had happened since then, but in Verity's eyes, no one had yet atoned for Bernie's needless death in the Benguela fire.

"I don't know what to think," she said. "Were it on personal regard alone, I should not hesitate in esteeming you very highly, Embrey, but—"

"Of course. The dreaded small print."

"Don't try and belittle it, damn you! For all I know, you and you father and uncle are the liars, and the Council acted appropriately. Ah, ah, not so fast." She stilled his vicious temper in mid-huff. "You asked the question, knowing how sensitive this topic is for both of us. So don't send for your second just yet. Let me finish. What I was trying to say was…inasmuch as your father's and your uncle's complicity in the rebel attack that killed my sister, I simply cannot take your word for their innocence. But nor shall I take their guilt for granted either, based on the findings of a court whose veracity is

177

now in question. I'm therefore reserving judgment on the Embrey family name."

His gaze softened, glazed. He looked away, cleared his throat—his manly pride at stake. "Which leaves your personal regard for me?"

"Aye. And yours for me." She widened her eyes, batted her lashes. "Tell me, am I all right in your book, Embrey?" Turning to give him a look at her side profile empowered her a little—other men had remarked on how striking it was.

He fidgeted, as though he were struggling to come up with the perfect response. "I say, fluky weather we're having."

"Very." *And fluky conversation.*

"Tell me. As a Gannet officer, at what point would you disobey an order from the powers-that-be?" he asked.

Again a moment of disorientation. His mercurial questions were really making her dizzy. "Pray clarify."

"It's just that, given the sheer ambition of the Council, as we've witnessed here—" he roved his hand over the mist in unison with his carefully chosen words, "—do you still consider yourself subject to its corrupt commands? Morally speaking?" He chewed his lip.

"I think I know what you're getting at, Embrey, and the answer is…probably not, no." *If father could hear me now!* "Before Bernie died, I daresay I would have followed any order to any end without thinking twice. That was what my father preached. The might of the empire was a force for good in the world, bringing light to the dark continent, etcetera. But when Bernie died, I *did* start to question why we were being asked to throw our lives away in countries so far from England we

178

could barely find them on the map. I followed orders, yes, but something changed inside me. I can't explain it. It was on the bottom of the English Channel when I finally felt—how can I put it?—expendable? Futile?"

"You'd surrendered yourself to a cause you no longer understood?"

"Yes, exactly. How did you—"

He nodded over the taffrail. "That was what my father said. He served in the colonial forces for years before his arrest. And in that one moment, despite his years of blind loyalty to a greater cause, he realized that devotion was not mutual. The empire cared nothing for those who truly sustained it— the workers, the troops, those who sacrificed the most and reaped the fewest rewards. He never profited a penny from those overseas ventures, and it didn't matter. They scapegoated him all the same."

"I don't care about rewards," she replied, "but I'd rather the Council explain exactly what it is they're up to building these towers around the world. It costs too many lives to sustain them. That's where they and I part company."

"Indeed. I'm glad."

"And after everything you and Professor Reardon have told me about the Council, I must admit it has shaken my trust somewhat."

She fidgeted, and found the seditious conversation curiously exciting. But why was her admission of mistrust so empowering? Father had always maintained the opposite was true—fighting for one's country was the ultimate source of pride.

"And what of you?" She determined the interrogation wasn't going to be completely one-sided.

179

And she didn't want to expose too much of her newfound rebelliousness in case he made her say something she'd regret. "What have you learned through all this, Embrey?"

"All this?"

"Hobnobbing with aeronauts, seeing life outside your fancy circles."

"What a bloody impertinent thing to say," he snapped.

She sighed. *Why can't I last two minutes without antagonising him?*

"But I tell you what I have learned." He demonstrated his freezing breath with a prolonged exhale.

"And that is?"

"That things happen for a reason. Take my daughter for instance. She inherits everything in the event of my disappearance."

Wait—what? How could he— "I—I didn't know you were married."

"I'm not. Never was. I knew Susan's mother only briefly in India before I returned home. When I found out she was with child, I offered to bring her to England and marry her, but she refused. Said she'd rather die than leave India. So I've provided for them both ever since. Funny how things work out, though, is it not? As soon as I'm declared extinct, little Susan will inherit one of the largest estates in England. It's in my will, and even if we make it back, I shan't lift a finger to stop it. With or without me, she ought to have my fortune. She barely knows me but...I'd dearly love to see her one last time."

"You're an honest fellow, Embrey."

He cleared his throat. "Speaking of which…and don't take this the wrong way, but…are *you* attached at all? In Africa, perhaps?"

"No." She shuddered through a sharp vision of Amyn lying weak in her arms, the poison squeezing the last drops of life from him. Strange, she hadn't thought of him for days, and he'd chosen this moment to distract her. She recoiled. "I believe we have more pressing concerns."

"Yes, indeed…like what's going to happen when we return." He rested his hands on the taffrail and then glimpsed her from the corner of his eye. "Forgive my impertinence—I realise this may be the farthest thing from your mind right now, given what we're about to attempt—but I'll not have it go unsaid any longer. We simply don't have time." He gazed wistfully out into the mist, then cleared his throat again. "Verity, when we return, would you consider accompanying me to Europe?"

"I would—" she answered without thinking, "—I mean what? Why? In what capacity?" *Could he be any vaguer? What does he want? A chaperone? Someone to sail him there and leave him? Another mistress? A* harlot?

"You know…to come with me," he replied evasively. "So we don't have to be apart."

"I see. And would I be playing the steamer trunk or the frock coat in this little pantomime?"

"Verity, I—"

She pressed a finger against his cold lips. "Unless you intend to court me, Embrey, don't speak another word. Not one more. I don't think I could take any more confounded uncertainty. Not here. Not now." A gap in the roving mist uncovered the hill of rubble outside

181

Reardon's factory. She let herself sink into Embrey's gentle embrace, the crinkling sound of his coat nestling against her both warm and sweet. A hint of tobacco enwrapped her.

"I intend to never let you go," he whispered.

She closed her eyes, rested her head on his shoulder, and felt the tension between them finally evaporate like the last icy dew of the Spring thaw. She opened her eyes. Through the fog, the sun tried to auger in a brilliant day but managed only a flaxen-silver glow. For the time being, all she had was hope, but it was enough.

"So you will go with me?"

"I will."

"Whatever happens?"

"Whatever happens," she promised.

Chapter 17

Harrison's Clock

First the smell of burning wood, then his favourite sensation, the warm steam wafting into his face, signalled Cecil's machine was ready to begin its cycle. He'd calibrated the Harrison clock and its sensitive psammeticum receptor—the Cavendish—as accurately as anything he'd ever measured. If the time jump didn't work, it would be through no fault of his own.

"You're sure we're standing close enough, Professor?" Verity Champlain shepherded her crewmen and women into a tighter group no more than fifteen feet from the brass clock. Tangeni and Embrey stood behind her, flanking young Billy Ransdell, who was without his dinosaur book for the first time in prehistory. Miss Polperro had insisted it be confiscated—a prudent move, even if it did make her seem even more like a horrid schoolmarm.

"Professor?" Verity asked.

"Yes, yes. Quite close enough."

"You said the original reaction was only supposed to send—what was it?—a plant pot a week into the future?"

Cecil patted her shoulder. "Yes, a potted plant, one week into the future. The reaction was meant to be localised, no more than a three foot radius. But I know now what enlarged the time bubble—moisture, first the steam inside the factory, then the rain outside. It acted as a conductor."

"So the whole factory's coming with us?"

"More than likely."

She raised an eyebrow, looked up, and then hurriedly put on her pith helmet for protection. "Well I have to hand it to you, Professor—you certainly don't do anything by half."

Cecil pretended he hadn't heard that, instead turned to watch the giant pistons drive the gears and cogs into that steady, almost pulse-like, thumping rhythm. "You can shove the rest of the coal in," he shouted to Kibo in the furnace room. "Then make sure you close the door. The boiler isn't quite at full steam."

"Understood."

A minute later, the engine man jogged back into the group. He received handshakes and back-slaps from his fellow aeronauts, then took his place behind the boy. A palpable anxiety etched itself on the faces of all gathered—lip-biting, worry lines deep and damp, gazes boring into Cecil at every hiss of steam from the juddery valves. These people expected. They demanded. This was to be his atonement.

He bowed his head and thought of poor Billy, orphaned by that first reckless attempt to conquer time; of the many Whitehall ministers and gentlemen of social standing he'd condemned to unspeakable deaths; of the brave African aeronauts who would never see home again; and mostly of his new friends, without whom he would not be standing here now, challenging God for a second time.

184

He looked up to the rickety old walkway shrouded in steam. The chair upon which he'd whiled away so many years was now empty and uninviting, like the hub of a long-abandoned, musty web. Lisa and Edmond were no longer up there, frozen in a still image, but with him instead, willing him to succeed. He had been selfish the first time, spiting fate without regard for the world around him. But the toils of many brave men and women had wrought this, his chance to make amends. This time jump was not for personal gain. It bore the blood of friends.

"Whatever happens, I'd like you all to know," he said, "I consider this my—"

Crack!

Blood peppered his face. Embrey careened into him and then slumped onto a secondary pipe. Before Cecil knew what had happened, he felt the hard muzzle of a rifle press against his temple.

"Don't move, Professor! Everything is going fine." The bastard's voice belonged to Carswell, Miss Polperro's number one crony. But what on earth was he *playing at?*

"Embrey!" Cecil reached for his friend but received a sharp kick to the back of his knee. He fell in a heap, the pain splintering up and down his leg. Verity and Tangeni backed away from Miss Polperro, whose crooked right arm appeared to point at something low in front of her. Three aeronauts lowering their rifles obstructed Cecil's view. He quickly scanned the throng.

"Where's Billy?" he asked.

"Don't worry, Professor. She won't shoot," Verity replied.

"Shoot? What is this?"

The aeronauts stepped aside to let him see…

Billy's tears streamed around the barrel of Miss Polperro's revolver pressed to his cheek. She wiped the steam from her spectacles. "Drop your weapons, aeronauts! I'll not ask again."

How in God's name did she get hold of him?

The crew turned to Verity, who widened her stance and placed her fists on her hips. "You'll do no such thing, men. Keep those rifles trained on the bitch's face. The boy ain't no bargaining chip."

"*Eembu,*" Tangeni stepped forward, "maybe we'd better—"

"Shut up. Step away. I'll take her out myself if I have to." Verity's glare intensified.

A wry curl of Agnes Polperro's lips signified her resolve. "By my reckoning we have less than five minutes before the machine has collected enough psammeticum to start refracting. At that point, the acceleration process is quick and exponential. So make up your minds. We either leave the boy behind as I suggested, or he dies. I'll not have his wayward fancies governing *my* destination. Now," she cocked the handgun, "decide among yourselves who stays with him. I care not."

Verity's furious glances appeared to take in the entire tableau in a matter of moments. She withdrew and crouched beside Embrey, whose side bled profusely. He would soon pass out.

"So you've thrown in with them, Kibo?" she said, sparking frantic chatter among the other aeronauts. "I have to admit, I didn't think you had it in you."

What? The engine man too? Cecil's jaw slackened when the well-dressed driver stepped forward, buttoning up his waistcoat. Had he snatched Billy for Polperro's posse? Had he armed the Whitehall gang?

"I'm sorry, *Eembu,* but she's right," Kibo said.

Tangeni aimed his scolding glare and forefinger at the traitor. "You're a dead man."

"You're wrong, brother. You're all wrong," the engine man replied. "Billy doesn't deserve this but you *have* to think of the greater good. We have enough uncertainties as it is without a boy's fancies dictating where we end up. We can all close our eyes, picture London and leave no doubt. But the boy is not to be trusted. The consequences are too dire to simply trust in him. You wouldn't see reason before, when this action could have been avoided, so you'll have to decide now instead. We've no time."

Cecil slapped Carswell's rifle away from his face and began crawling toward the Harrison clock. "I'm stopping it," he said. "Go ahead, shoot me instead. I dare you."

He hadn't traversed the first pipe when Carswell yanked him back by his sore leg. "You'll pay for that." Cecil pulled himself the few feet along the secondary brass pipe until he reached Embrey. The butt of a steam-pistol peeked out from the young man's jacket. Verity saw that Cecil had seen and gave him a quick wink.

Yes. Everything in our power. Let them *stop us if they must.*

He snatched one steam-pistol from Embrey's belt and Verity snatched the other. Cecil spun and shot up repeatedly at Carswell, each bullet piercing his torso until the bushy-eyebrowed swine spat blood. All hell broke loose in the shadow of the machine. Verity spent most of her bullets trying to hit Kibo, but the engine man darted for cover behind old Kincaid, using him as a human shield. The elder statesman, shot through the heart, slumped lifeless.

Meanwhile, Tangeni sneaked around the back of them and wrestled Kibo.

The two officers went at it hammer and tongs. Kibo was the bigger man but not the tougher. After he ducked a huge roundhouse punch, Tangeni leapt in and jabbed his opponent's windpipe, crushing his airway. The traitor fell to the floor and choked slowly in the grease and grime, his waistcoat torn and soiled.

Across the factory, the aeronauts and Miss Polperro's cronies had each other pinned down, the latter group boasting more weapons than anyone had guessed. Kibo had to have armed them. Their bullets ricocheted off water casks and brass scaffolding. Cecil couldn't tell who was who.

"Professor, can you stand?" Verity knelt over Embrey.

Cecil struggled to one knee, then braced his sore leg. His adrenaline seemed to dilute the pain. "Yes, I think so."

"Then *here*." She threw him her pistol. "For God's sake, shut this machine down. Kill anyone who tries to stop you."

"What about you?"

"I'm getting Embrey back to the *Empress*. He'll die if I can't remove this bull—"

A tremendous crash shook the factory. The thudding of collapsed masonry and metal brought with it a plaster cloud thick enough to envelop the gunfight and obscure the opposing sides from each another. Cecil looked first to the boiler room. Had that exploded? No, there was no billowing steam. What then?

The firing ceased. Loose bricks clinked one on top the other as they fell somewhere near the front entrance, while the hiss of settling plaster dust wrought quiet tension in this lull in the fighting.

"Be careful, Professor. But hurry." Verity turned from the cloud and wasted no more time in dragging Embrey over two pipes and behind the left hand piston. From there, she had a straight path to daylight. Cecil prayed she had some surgical knowledge too—removing a bullet wasn't something one could or should muddle through.

A queer squelching, grinding noise emerged from inside the cloud.

"God, what's that smell?" someone yelled.

As the next *thump, thump* trembled the ground, sounding as though it was shifting piles of bricks already fallen, Cecil rolled up his sleeves. He prepared for a last desperate attempt to stop his machine. For time wasn't just running out, it had come calling…stalking. Summoned by the gunshots.

The baryonyx!

Its giant snout pierced the cloud before the first screams erupted from the Whitehall posse. Its jaws gaped for a vicious lunge into the cornered men, then snapped shut upon two, hurtling them aloft for a fuller bite. The crunching and squelching resumed at a sickening volume. Gunshots from both sides, designed to ward off the baryonyx, merely enraged it further. Its crocodilian mouth beslobbered with fresh blood now thrust even lower, even quicker.

Cecil spied the Harrison clock's brass lid vibrating as it dripped moisture. The final accelerating process was

189

about to begin. He climbed the first pipe, smacked his sore leg on the second. Those angry cogs and crank wheels were no longer rotating numbered dials—the machine already had her sequence, her key to unlock time. They were powering the energy transfer itself, the unleashing of built-up psammeticum into the intricate array of mirrors, and the boldest clockwork ever devised.

He spun to make sure the dinosaur was not following.

A sudden blow to his jaw sent him reeling. Delaney, another of the lynchers from the first night, picked him up and thumped his gut. Cecil coughed, struggled to breathe. A few feet away, Miss Polperro shook Billy by the scruff of his neck and glowered at Cecil.

"You're full of surprises, Reardon," she hissed. "But I warned you what would happen. Say goodbye to this boy. It's for all our sakes."

A tiny dark shape emerged from her matted hair. It rushed across her brow. She recoiled and then shook her head. It shifted again, this time with a speed and scurrying motion Cecil recalled from his recent past.

The spider from the platform.

It stopped on her right temple and must have bitten her, for she shrieked and let go of the boy. The baryonyx answered, its rage deafening the entire factory.

Cecil lunged forward and knocked the revolver from her hand. Billy wriggled free and bolted for safety. *Run lad, run.* Delaney snatched the steam-pistol from the ground. Frantic, Cecil scrabbled for the second weapon somewhere on the floor. He found it between the bastard's legs and immediately fired up into his groin. *Click.* An empty cartridge! Instead, he thumped his attacker's kneecap with the pistol butt, felling him. He cracked the brass gun against Delaney's forehead with all his might. The son of a bitch went out like a gaslight.

More screams and gunshots from behind, but also from the front, as well. From outside. *Verity and Embrey.* He heard other voices too.

He made straight for the clock with seconds to spare. He felt the prickly warmth caused by the hurtling, expanding energy. Every hair on his body stood up. A flicker of lilac light appeared through an old screw hole in the brass casing. He unclasped one side, reached for the other. An extraordinary wrench in his scalp pulled him back. It was as though his hair had burst into flames.

A frightful witch clawed at him, her metal spectacles aglow with lilac light. Her shock of hair resembled a penny dreadful cartoon of Sweeny Todd he'd seen in his youth. At once, the hate broiling in her eyes seemed to encapsulate the very thing he'd railed against all these years. Death. That vicious, remorseless force behind the taking of innocent lives: Billy's, Lisa's, Edmond's…

He wrestled her to arm's length and, summoning all his hate, delivered an uppercut to her jaw with such force it felt as though his fist was made of iron. Her head snapped back, then she flopped at his feet.

"Cecil!" The boy ran to him, flung his arms around him.

"Hold tight, Billy." Cecil picked the lad up and, calmly inside a torrent of inverted lilac rain, held him like he'd once held Edmond.

"What should I do?" Billy's dampened words slurred with unearthly resonance, as though time itself were stretching them.

"Think of home, son. Just think of—"

Everything vanished in a blinding flash.

Chapter 18

Cause and Caprice

The second journey through time seemed to pass through an ocean of perpetual, curdled milk. Trapped with Cecil in that timeless, soundless oyster was the sum total of all the hopes and horrors his adventure had fed into the machine: befriending and losing his two sterling companions, Embrey and Verity; saving Billy, the very boy he'd made an orphan with his first time jump; the hideous, engorged baryonyx wreaking havoc in his factory; falling victim to Miss Polperro's treachery; but also besting those myriad prehistoric hazards to repair his great machine. When all was said and done, even if he could never fully atone for ripping the heart out of London, he'd at least kept his word and conjured this second chance for everyone.

What happened next was out of his hands.

As the whiteness dulled, noises around the factory staggered in repetition as though time's needle were stuck on a glitchy gramophone disc. Billy's arms slipped from around Cecil's waist. A draught whistled overhead, tossing dust. He coughed, then spun at the first uninterrupted roar this side of the time jump. Whenever here was.

Enraged, the barynoyx rampaged toward the aeronauts on the north side of the factory. It crushed one of the primary steam pipes, and backed away from the ensuing hot exhaust. Meanwhile, the aeronauts bolted for the rubble at the back of the factory, while the Whitehall posse—what was left of them—made for the front doors from whence the dinosaur had entered. It made after the latter group, probably following their coughs inside the dust cloud. But as it turned, its massive tail smashed into a primary piston shank. The impact uncoupled one of the steel scaffold supports, and the whole thing began to buckle, to topple…

With his injured leg, Cecil could never climb the pipes in time.

"Get away, Billy!" He grabbed the lad under his arms and hurled him sideways as far and as high as he could. Billy landed on the nearest pipe, his momentum sliding him over the other side.

Tonnes of brass and iron crushed Cecil's trailing leg as he tried to escape. It hit with the pain of a thousand kiln burns all at once, and held him there, in hell, until his cry exhausted the air in his lungs. Then he cried again. The last thing he saw before he blacked out was the grim, desperate face of his African friend, Tangeni, as the redoubtable aeronaut picked his way through the twisted wreckage of the time machine.

"Professor? Can you hear me? Professor?" A familiar voice—affected English, oddly enunciated vowels, almost amusing. "Professor Reardon?"

"Tangeni?"

He hadn't been moved from the spot where he'd fallen, nor had the sweaty smell of soot and steam

194

dissipated, nor could he yet tell to which destination the time machine had brought them. It was dark outside, beyond the mess of pipes and beams. A dozen black faces huddled in a semi-circle over him, greeting his gaze with either smiles or puzzled frowns. Tangeni's torch flame lent the aeronauts a magnificent, mysterious air, as though they were indeed from another time, another world from Cecil's.

"We all glad you okay, Professor," one of the younger men said, an apprentice in Kibo's engine room if Cecil recalled. "Billy and me—we make you up some sarsaparilla. It no longer fizz, but it still good." He handed Cecil the cup.

"Thank you, young man." When he tried to sit up, Cecil felt a tear in his right leg that knocked him sick. He yelped in pain and couldn't stop coughing.

"Here. You need to drink something." Tangeni pressed the cup to his lips, poured in a mouthful of sarsaparilla. "You're badly hurt, Professor. The piston pinned your leg to the floor, almost severed it. I tied it with a tourniquet and the bleeding has stopped. But you're in poor shape, I'm afraid. Reba and Philomena, they have gone for help. But *Eembu* taught me to always be honest in times like these—I think that whatever happens, you have lost that leg, Professor. Nothing can be done."

Cecil shivered coldly, clasped Tangeni's hand. Such terrible news and yet he took it well, only a vague regret of never being able to ride a penny farthing—something he'd always wanted to try but had never quite got around to—aching his heart. *Punchdrunk priorities.*

"Billy? Where's Billy?"

"'Ere, Cecil. How are you feelin'?" The lad was watching from Cecil's left, chin on hands atop a buckled beam.

"Like I've just slid down the biggest snake on the board."

After a pause, "You can 'ave another throw if you like. You 'ave as many as you want."

"Much obliged." Sweet boy. Saving him from the clutches of Agnes Polperro had been a proud moment, one he would never forget. *Speaking of which…*

"Where *is* that she-devil?"

"Gone. Soon after the baryonyx left, one of her cronies woke up. I think it was the one you knocked cold, Professor." Delaney. Tangeni had seen a lot. "He carried Miss Polperro out, that way." He pointed at the front entrance. "Out into the centre of London."

"Excuse me? Did you say—"

"Yeah, we did it, Cecil." A note of barely-restrained defiance lifted Billy's voice. "We proved that old witch wrong after all. It were nothin'. I pictured Embrey runnin' there in the rain, right before 'e got into our car. That were just before the first time jump. It were easy. I could do it again any time, no problem."

"So we're back in London? The very same night?" He couldn't believe what he was hearing. Time-wise, they'd found the correct grain of salt on a sandy beach at night…in a hurricane?

"Not the same night, no," Tangeni replied. "It is dry outside. No storm. And if this were even soon after the original time jump, would not the whole area be swarming with panicked people? With police? The military?"

"You're right there, Tangeni."

196

The African waved his torch away to the west, toward the centre of London. "It is only the factory and ourselves made it back. *Eembu* and Embrey, they—"

"I know. We lost them. *I* lost them, my friend."

Tangeni held his head high, his bottom lip quivering.

"But I can get them back too." Cecil didn't have an inkling of how he might accomplish that feat, but the determination felt so inviolate inside every fibre of his being that he knew he'd either achieve it or die trying. Verity and Embrey had given him his chance to make amends, to return the survivors to London. They'd granted him this victory over time and over fate. Now it was his turn to repay the debt—a debt borne deep in his heart, for they would never be nearer *and* farther from him than they were at this moment.

He began to shiver uncontrollably. The faint sound of a dog barking reminded him where they were, what might be coming—the full wrath of the Leviacrum. It was time to think of the future.

"Tangeni, will you do what I ask? We don't have much time."

"Aye, Professor. Whatever you ask."

"Is the Harrison Clock still intact, or is it crushed?"

"The Harris—"

"The device inside the cylindrical casing, a few feet behind you."

Wavering firelight. Shuffling feet. Hushed voices. "It is still intact."

"Very well. Good. I need you to unclasp the lid on both sides, and then unscrew the nickel wheel casings from the device inside."

More whispering. A collective effort from sharp, capable minds light-years out of their milieu. Scraping, squeaking metal. "Done, Professor."

"Good, Tangeni, good. Now lift the device out and wrap it in a coat or something. Two coats, three, to make sure."

"What shall we do with it?" Concern, rather than inquisitiveness sharpened Tangeni's question.

Cecil's every muscle began to tingle, to fade from his control. He knew his life was leaving him. But there was still a chance for Embrey and Verity.

"I need you to…take it to Professor Sorensen in Tromso." His eyes eased closed of their own accord. "Make note of the sequence of numbers on the exposed dial…the one with ten digits. Make sure Professor Sorensen gets…that number." The last embers of his life seemed to melt into fizzy liquid and leak out from his outstretched fingertips. "For Billy," he whispered. "Look after Billy. Always watch out for…for Billy."

"I will, Professor. I swear it."

"Go now. Protect my secret. Go and best time…one last time. Save the young heir and…and his air maiden from…"

A dog barked again, closer this time. It sounded like Leonard, his bandy-legged bulldog he'd loved as a boy. He smiled, contented. If Leonard was there waiting for him, maybe Lisa and Edmond were waiting there too.

Maybe…

Chapter 19

Phantasmagoria

Already a pungent, scorched-earth smell spread from the factory, and the hairs on her arms and the back of her neck bristled as Verity dragged Embrey outside over the rubble. The cold and the damp mist had subsided a little. She could see the *Empress* clearly. Embrey stirred, groaned and then doubled up in agony, the bullet wound in his side leaking more blood than she'd like.

"Here." She removed her scarf and bunched it to the size of a fist. "Keep this pressed to the wound, no matter how much it hurts." Helping him to his feet, she tried to blank his suffering and the deafening volleys of gunfire from her mind—her one concern now was to get him to her cabin and remove the bullet. But the scorched-earth smell hadn't dissipated, and the charged air remained bristly and potent. Reardon had better get a move on. Maybe she should have stayed with him until he shut the blasted thing down after all. Maybe she should go back now and see it through...

A gigantic, muscular bulk lumbered out of the mist ahead, as big as a tram and twice as heavy. The baryonyx positioned itself between her and the airship, its massive tail whipping the steel deck ladder, almost yanking it off its tethers. The dinosaur turned to see what had made the clanging noise, then scraped its teeth along the starboard bulwark.

Now or never.

Verity made for the tri-wheel, urging Embrey to keep as quiet as he could while she supported his limp frame. Her stealth lasted but a moment. A gunshot rang out from the rubble behind, and two panicked, middle-aged Whitehall men dashed for the tri-wheel. One of them fired again at the baryonyx. Reckless, insane. The dinosaur thrust its crocodilian jaw around at forty-five degrees and unleashed a terrifying roar.

"You bloody fools." She hissed as they tried to toss Embrey aside from the vehicle. One of them climbed in, frantically started up the steam engine. The other yanked her hair and kicked Embrey to the ground, desperate to gain the passenger seat.

Enough was enough.

Furious, she jabbed the second man's throat and pulled him out by the scruff of his neck. He coughed hard but swung even harder—his fist to Verity's gut left her bent double. The baryonyx stalked through the mud, drawn by the frantic action. In a few moments it would be upon them, and Embrey! He'd collapsed again and was shivering on his side. Whatever happened she had to get him inside the tri-wheel.

Luckily the first man had made a hash of operating the valves, his curses generating more heat than anything inside the steam engine. The second man did his best to fend Verity off with kicks but she seized his legs and dragged him off the passenger seat. As if to avenge his lunkheadedness at the controls, the driver immediately leapt to his colleague's aid across the seats. He swung a vicious punch at Verity. She ducked, dealt him a quick uppercut, then planted a terrific boot on his kneecap. The bone cracked. She leapt to one side. As he bent to nurse his wound, she quickly raised her right leg as high it would go and then brought the heel down with wrecking force upon the back of his neck. A deadly blow she'd learned from Amyn's brother in Zanzibar.

The man crumpled beside Embrey. His colleague had seen enough. He scrambled to his feet in the mud and made a beeline for the factory. Giant, swinging rows of daggers caught him mid-stride and plucked him screaming into the air. The baryonyx tossed him and chewed him for a few moments before its mighty tail whipped round against the tri-wheel, knocking it onto its side. The vehicle crushed the unconscious Whitehall man and narrowly missed Embrey.

Verity crouched behind the overturned car at his side, heart a'gallop. Any kind of movement now—even though Embrey was running out of time—would be suicide. The dinosaur didn't appear to notice her. She covered Embrey's mouth with her palm to quell his groans.

The air heated, thickened all of a sudden, as though a tropical summer heatwave had bled through the wintry chill. She found it hard to breathe. Blue sparks leapt from Embrey's skin to her fingertips.

As she looked up, the baryonyx lumbered away up the side of the factory, skirting a pale, lilac glow.

"Oh my God. Not yet!"

A crackle from behind drew her gaze. Purple light snaked up from the ground onto the lines of the *Empress,* and shot around her envelopes and cables like St. Elmo's Fire run amok. *Christ, here we go.* Verity was sure the time bubble had spread too far once again. It would envelop

201

the entire area, not just the factory. Any moment now, London would reform around the ruins, the airship would find herself afloat on the Thames, and everything would be fine.

The end of her world came swiftly, in the flicker of a gaslight. She turned and heard a waspish buzz and saw the mirage of a great city through obsidian glass where the factory should be. A web-like bubble of white-purple light swelled, intensified from its base to its crown, then wavered like a giant candle flame in a heavenly draught. In an instant it was gone. The bubble. The factory. The light.

No farewell. Nothing.

Oh God.

A cold vice, colder and more crushing than the deepest suit dive, froze her heart. Slivers of lilac light floated and spiralled down through the empty space as fizzing leaves and spinning jennies. None of them reached the ground, instead evaporated with gentle crackles. All around the site, wisps of steam gathered on the faint outline of a sphere and then faded away.

She gazed up at Big Ben. Its clock face read five past eight. She dabbed a sleeve on her brow, trying to wipe a little reality into her shocking new world but it was too sudden, too impossible. The clock had read five past eight over a week ago, when they'd first arrived. From now on, it would *always* read that time.

The baryonyx paced around the far side of the vanished light-show, questing through the empty, adjacent buildings. Verity shook the bitter fog from her brain and turned her attentions back to saving Embrey—a battle she at least knew how to fight. Hell,

202

she'd helped pluck bullets out of wounded men and women before…in a past life…

The baryonyx stalked through the empty ruins all through the evening, perhaps fascinated by the extraordinary smell left in the wake of the time jump. Acrid and sooty, it reminded her of bonfire night. When it left, a pack of curious dromaeosaurs pottered about the site. She watched them from Embrey's bedside in her cabin, a rifle stood against the window sill for protection.

Though she'd retrieved the bullet and a tiny fragment of his shirt, he'd contracted a vicious fever. His pale skin dripped with perspiration, and every now and then she dabbed his brow with a damp cloth. The more he muttered insensibly, the clearer she glimpsed her end— the loneliest end imaginable, millions of years from another soul. She'd been a fool to let *anyone*—even her own men—near Billy or Reardon. If she'd managed it more prudently, where would they be right now? Was the city she'd glimpsed really London? If Reardon was still alive, would he ever come back for them?

There was always a chance.

"If you ever make it to Piccadilly, Tangeni…" she lay Billy's dinosaur book next to her glass of brandy on the desk, "be sure to buy the boy an ice cream."

She stared out into prehistory as one confined to its savage isolation forever. If only things had turned out differently. If only.

"*Enda nawa,* my friend. *Enda nawa.*"

One week later…

An eager easterly breeze prodded the balloons overhead while she paced about A-deck, tracing cables and rails with her fingertips as though it might reawaken precious memories of her adventures in the corps. But the *Empress* was a ghost ship. Her spirit had departed with Tangeni and the last of the aeronauts. Verity would fly her as far and as long as she was able, and when her gas was spent, the Gannet would slowly rust and crumble with the rest of man's anachronisms. Bleak, yes, but she had served her purpose. She had kept enough of her crew alive to enable the return trip through time. Whatever else happened, she had at least done that.

"You finished yet?" she called to Embrey, who'd been writing in his blasted journal for hours. Verity had prepared the boiler and secured the water barrels and salted the meat and made enough hydrogen to buoy the balloons for days, and still she waited for him. "You'd better not have writer's cramp. You've a boiler to stoke, Dickens."

"Has the wind changed, then?" he hollered.

"Changed and sick of waiting for you."

A clatter and a growl emerged from her cabin, and he appeared from beneath the steps looking trim and handsome in his waistcoat. He rolled up his shirtsleeves. "A hundred million years and still I get no peace. That's women for you."

Fists on hips, she glared playfully at him. "If it's peace you're after, I can arrange a lasting one. Now haul your backside to the engine room, Marquess."

"Yes, ma'am. And may I have permission to see you in your cabin later?"

"That depends."

"On what?"

"On what kind of stoking you have in mind." She blew him a kiss. He caught it and held it against his heart.

When they were airborne, Embrey returned to the quarterdeck wheel and, hand in hand, they both steered the ship ahead of the wind, away from London-that-was, perhaps for the last time. Geyser clouds shrouded the way east, but without the weight of a diving bell and a crew, the *Empress* quickly rose higher than she'd ever climbed before.

"Quatermain would be proud." Embrey treated her to a slow, tender kiss that lifted her heavenward. "Although…he never liked to fly."

"And you?"

His grin eased to a gentle smile, and he gazed reflectively at the horizon. "Didn't you know? I was high-born to start with."

She snuggled up to him while they watched the clouds sail by.

Chapter 20

A Posthumous Pardon

"He's the key to it all, Agnes. I think he always was—the loss of his wife and son turned him against everything and everyone. We've seen it time and again, greatness lying dormant until a person is visited by profound adversity. Nothing rouses creativity like a personal challenge. In his case, a challenge from Fate unlocked some deep, miraculous vault in his brain. He may have done it for love or for hate, or for the thing that drives all men to trample his fellow men."

"What's that?"

"Power. The power mankind has sought ever since it first began to question its limitations. The power we are destined, ultimately, to achieve, if we survive that long without destroying ourselves. At the moment, God alone possesses it, and we are but the dazzled viewers glimpsing it through His heavenly nickelodeon."

"Blasphemy!"

"No, Agnes. I don't believe that. No, I see it as blasphemy to deny man his rightful ascendancy. If the Leviacra stand for anything, it is for the limitlessness of our potential. God himself made us this way, with the gift of evolution. He *wants* us to rise above our antecedents until we are subject to no law or force beyond our control. We may have only glimpsed the vastness of that potential so far, but I firmly believe we are close to filling that glimpse with an entirely new perception of how the universe works, the way the slenderest beam of light might shine through a crack into an untouched sanctum, illuming little but hinting at immeasurable opportunity. Reardon has lit the torch, Agnes. He *must* join our ranks, but he must never—"

On the far side of his grogginess, the sound of a key fiddling in its lock suddenly confirmed what Cecil had been wrestling with. He had not died. He was not dead. The notion peeled away several layers of mental skin he'd grown during a forever sleep. How long had he been out? He was too weak to open his eyes. But the voices he'd been listening to in his dream were not from a dream after all. Agnes? Agnes Polperro? Was that harpy standing over him right now, with someone, a high-up in the Council?

"Is he—" Another familiar, male voice began.

"You know, I think he just might be!" The garrulous man kept his reply to a vociferous whisper, but Cecil's hearing was uncommonly acute, a phenomenon often experienced by those who wake after sleeping for long periods. "Stay with him, Wallingford. As soon as he's lucid, reassure him. Confide in him. You and Agnes have my full confidence."

"Yes, sir," said the man who'd just entered.

"Thank you, sir," said Miss Polperro.

Quiet footsteps across what sounded like linoleum. The key in the lock. More whispering, this time impossible to discern. Lorne Wallingford, government minister, member of the Whig cabinet? Agnes Polperro, Leviacrum representative, bitch responsible for banishing Embrey and Verity to prehistory? The man

207

who'd just left had spoken like one of those uppity university bods, part scientist, part philosopher, all windbag. But anyone in a position to delegate to Wallingford had serious clout. This had to be somewhere away from public scrutiny, most likely inside the Leviacrum tower itself. Perhaps the infirmary floor.

"Professor Reardon?"

He rolled his head on the pillow, swallowed repeatedly until the saliva gave his dry, flaky throat some semblance of lubrication. The unpleasant metallic taste almost made him retch. He moved his fingers, then the toes in his left foot. His right foot…didn't respond. He yawned, mashed his eyes closed before opening them with tender, jittery blinks. It took minutes for them to become accustomed to the medium light in the infirmary ward. An empty ward—his was the only bed, and but for handsome landscape paintings adorning the pale blue walls it was a bare, depressing room, far too big for its current one-patient function. He felt marooned somehow, left behind by all that was good in the world. Then a prick of self-importance tickled him, and he recalled the almost reverential manner in which the mysterious overseer had spoken of him to Agnes Polperro.

Yes, he had something they wanted. Wanted badly. The secret to large-scale time travel—a bargaining chip he might use to procure all sorts of things. And then there were his friends…

What happened to Billy? Tangeni? The others? Did they make it to Tromso?

"We're very glad you've recovered, Professor Reardon." Wallingford's crooked back and hawkish stare reminded Cecil of a rhamphorhynchus, a small, prehistoric lizard-like bird with a hideous countenance.

"I'm—" he swallowed the dryness once more, "—I'm not."

"Oh, come now, sir. You are the most talked-about man in all the empire—nay, the world. To us here in the Leviacrum, your achievement has outstripped that of any scientist who ever lived. Surely that is worth waking up to."

Cecil didn't respond. This feeble buttering-up preamble wasn't worthy of such a noted diplomat as Wallingford—it reeked of desperation.

"We'll get straight to the point, then." Miss Polperro pressed the bridge of her thick-rimmed spectacles higher up her nose and strode forward. Her chin still bore the dark print of his uppercut, but the bruise had healed somewhat. He guessed a week had passed. "I make no apologies for my actions in the prelude to the time jump, Professor, as I still maintain, no matter how it turned out, that having the boy accompany us was too great a risk. In my opinion we were lucky."

She nursed the bruise on her chin with a handkerchief.

"That being said, I never meant you personally any ill-will during our time spent in prehistory, as any witness will attest. No, my sole preoccupation was to return as many British residents as possible to our own time, and that we achieved together, Professor. While you reassembled your machine, I ensured the men in my charge remained alive and motivated. We may have clashed on a technicality, but I want you to know that I hold you in the highest esteem as both a scientist and a gentleman. Whatever transpired during those weeks

209

adrift in time *after* the initial cataclysm, you have little to reproach yourself over. In fact you have earned the utmost respect of the Council."

Careful words designed to divorce his culpability from his achievement. Cecil sensed they were about to focus on the latter, while the former would be glossed over. Good news and bad news apportioned with guile, packaged for surreptitious ends—politics at work if ever he'd heard it.

He lifted his head a fraction, enough to see to the foot of his bed. Again, only his left toes responded. Recalling the awful weight pinning his right leg in the factory and Tangeni's words—"Whatever happens, you have lost that leg, Professor. Nothing can be done"—he reached down under the blanket. The smooth, metallic surface shocked him for a moment. It began part way down his thigh and clearly represented a full, artificial limb—under cover, the foot appeared equal in size to his natural left one.

"How long was I unconscious?" he asked, to distract from the shocking new revelation.

"In a coma for two days, sedated for a further four. But you'll want to see what Professor Sorensen has invented for you." Before Cecil could protest, Miss Polperro peeled back the blanket to reveal his newfangled perambulatory gift. He tried shutting his eyes but it was no use. He *had* to know.

A shiny brass leg shaped in every way like a human one, with a complex knee joint governed by gears and levers, it was both a monstrosity and thing of unparalleled beauty. Extraordinary care and craftsmanship had wrought it, not to mention an ingenuity far surpassing any artificial appendages he'd ever seen or read about. Sorensen had always been brilliant but this almost defied belief.

"When you are well again our technicians will instruct you on how to walk on it." She tapped the metal shin with her knuckles. A slight vibration tickled his upper thigh.

Wallingford stepped forward, thumbing his lapels. "We would also like to invite you to join our most elite committee, the Atlas Club, wherein you will immediately be appointed to the Leviacrum Council itself. Such is our regard for your splendid accomplishments, Professor Reardon. What say you, sir?"

Fear the Greeks bringing gifts.

"Not unconditional, I presume." Cecil knew.

Wallingford pouted, rocked on his heels as he cleared his throat. "I'm afraid not. As pardonable as the destruction of Westminster may be to us in the Council in light of the scope of its ramifications for science, the British people are demanding that you face trial for the most serious capital offences. If we were to hand you over to the judicial system, if you were to set foot outside this tower, you would hang, Professor. Of that there is no doubt."

"No, I don't doubt it either." And he'd already been hung once. Not his jolliest memory. "So your offer is to spare my life in exchange for the secret I possess. That right?"

"You put it succinctly, sir, but yes, that is what we propose. You would continue your work in the laboratories and hopefully not only emulate your great achievement but refine it as well, with the full resources of the Leviacrum and all its eminent scientists at your disposal. You would be the spearhead of humanity's conquest of time itself. For that, we guarantee your inclusion in every decision governing the use of time travel, and also complete autonomy in any future endeavours you wish to pursue.

"But you can never again leave this tower, and no civilian may be permitted to visit you. Only those who already work in the tower will have that privilege. Would that that were flexible, Professor, but I'm afraid the Council has insisted upon its strict im—"

Wallingford froze, his contorted lips set to wrap around the next syllable, still as a clay figurine. His eyes didn't blink. Not even the subtle rocking of the posture one can always discern if he scrutinizes a still-life actor closely enough. No, the crookbacked politician had quite literally, insensibly, been petrified!

What the hell?

The hands on the clock on the far wall were not moving. Very odd. Nor were the shadows of passing clouds dimming the room even slightly. He craned his neck to peer out through the large porthole windows. There were clouds but no movement, birds but no progress through the sky, distant airships as still as dead, swatted flies stuck to a great blue mural.

He massaged his aching frown with his forefinger and thumb. Either he was still dreaming after all, or something profoundly wrong had just occurred.

"At five past eight, twice a day, Professor." Miss Polperro waved her hand in front of Wallingford's face, eliciting no reaction. So why wasn't *she* affected?

"I think we'd be wise to keep it to ourselves," she said, "until we can fathom the cause. It is a most peculiar thing—it began the day we arrived back, and the survivors of the time jump appear to be the only ones

212

free to move about inside this…glitch in time. We are the only ones immune. Now, say nothing of it, for it lasts for only forty-one seconds each time. That is no great hardship." She checked her pocketwatch, then shuffled back to her original position. "Remember, twice a day at five past eight. Be ready for it."

"I'll…I will." Cecil gazed at the Madame Tussaud's politician, waiting for a sudden reanimation. When it came, there was that stutter again, time's needle stuck on its gramophone disc, that he'd experienced as 1908 had manifested after the latest time jump.

"—plementation. There can be no exception to that." Wallingford resumed as though nothing had happened. Indeed, from his point of view, nothing *had* happened.

Cecil lay back, took several deep breaths. The more he considered that idea of the gramophone needle and the circular disc, the more it seemed to fit this bizarre phenomenon. Somehow, the rip in time had caused this glitch. If each day were considered a revolution of time, then five past eight, when they'd originally departed for the Cretaceous, was the damaged moment—the time at which 1908 stuck, twice daily, like the needle upon the scratched disc. Had it recurred here like clockwork all the while they'd been away? If so, no one would have known, just as they didn't now. Only the time travellers were aware of it, remained unaffected by it.

Extraordinary.

"Perhaps we should give you a chance to think over our proposal, Professor Reardon?" Wallingford touched his earlobe as he glanced at Miss Polperro—a signal for them to leave. "When you're better rested perhaps?"

"No, that's quite all right. You can have my answer now. I agree to all your terms, and I will gladly join your Atlas Council or whatever the blasted thing is called. But I would like three things in return."

The curious tilt of Wallingford's head betrayed his genuine surprise. Had he not expected to discuss terms so soon? All the better. "Yes?" he asked.

Gritting his teeth, Cecil half sat up and bunched his pillow behind him against the brass bars at the head of his bed. "Firstly, unconditional, posthumous pardons must be given to Lord Garrett Embrey, his father, Marquess Embrey, and his uncle, Lord Fitzwalter. The highest military service commendation must go to Lieutenant Verity Champlain and her second in command, Lieutenant Tangeni. All these must be announced in the *Times* before I even think about resuming work."

The crookbacked politician's fake smile barely masked his chagrin. "I believe that can be arranged, but—"

"Secondly, I demand to know why Embrey's family was victimized."

"That one I can answer personally," Wallingford said. "Both his father and uncle were highly influential men, in business and in politics. We gave them an invitation to join the Atlas Club, along with a brief explanation of its purpose, and they refused. In today's seditious climate, such a refusal cast doubt upon their loyalty to the Crown. After the Benguela fire, we thought it prudent to make an example of aristocratic officers for a change, to remind our armed forces that no one, no matter their station or privilege, is above the law."

"So you hanged two innocent men?"

"For the greater good, yes. It wasn't the first time and it won't be the last. In every country it has long been a vital method of ensuring general obedience during wartime."

"Tried and tested or not, it's repugnant. Not to mention evil."

"If you can come up with a better way, Professor, be my guest."

Cecil narrowed his eyes at the little bastard. "Just give me that chance."

Miss Polperro's angry scoff only redoubled his grit. "Why not appoint yourself Prime Minister while you're at it." She paced to the far wall, chuntering to herself.

"Ha! And thirdly, I want you two to summarize for me, here and now, the grand purpose behind these godforsaken towers that reach for the clouds for no apparent reason." He glared at Wallingford, who sniffled and checked his pocketwatch. "Is that too much to ask?" He filled those words with as much scorn as he could manage—not as much as he'd hoped, for curiosity had got the better of him. He'd longed to know the answer to this riddle for most of his life. He'd even worked in the tower for many years without having so much as an inkling as to why it had been built in the first place.

Wallingford blinked rapidly, no doubt considering all the angles before formulating his response, as all political creatures are wont to do. "Very well, Professor. A brief summary you shall have. I'm quite certain the other Council members would not begrudge you that *if* you accede to our request." His sharp glance across to his schoolmarm colleague met with a bitter, resigned shrug.

Well, well. How the tables have turned. It seems I do have the winning hand after all.

"How much do you know of the Atlas comets?" Wallingford asked.

"Little except the name." *Comets? Whatever next?*

"They are three comets of varying mass, whose wide, unusual orbits around our sun occasionally bring them within close proximity to the earth."

"Yes, I saw a painting once," Cecil said. "The 1714 comet shower—lit the western sky with brilliant blue sparks for a full day and night."

"Correct, but do you know what the blue sparks actually were?"

"Hmm, I'll hazard a guess at highly concentrated psammeticum in either solid or gaseous form."

"Very good, Professor." Miss Polperro unhooked the clock from his wall and hurled it against the skirting board, sending clockwork innards and glass smithereens all across the floor. The crash spun Wallingford around. A moment later he began to chuckle, and Miss Polperro grinned at him. Some kind of private joke they shared, one Cecil would rather not be in on.

And she called me mentally unstable!

"Three comets, two imminent encounters with the earth," she said. Her little colleague bowed in acquiescence to her scientific expertise. "The next encounter, in two years' time, will be similar to that of 1714. We plan to channel a significant amount of psammeticum directly into the tower, at high altitude. Its gaseous form is diluted in a high oxygen atmosphere, so by the time it reaches the earth's surface, it has lost much of its potency. By collecting it in a slightly thinner

216

air, we will conserve an enormous amount of psammeticum energy."

"Yes, I know *that*. The spire receptor has been gathering it for years."

"Only the cosmic trickle—trifling amounts."

"So how much are we talking about? These comets you speak of?"

"That's classified." She glanced at Wallingford, who merely rolled his eyes. "The comets' second close pass, in a decade's time, will shower the earth with approximately five times that amount," she said. "By then, our towers will be significantly higher, our storage units more sophisticated. We will be able to stockpile an extraordinary volume of psammeticum, approximately a trillion times that which we currently collect from the meagre cosmic trickle. So you see, Professor, why these great edifices reach for the sky."

He scrubbed his face with weak, aching hands. "Admirable, but why all the secrecy?"

"Why, exclusivity of course. If our enemies got wind of it, they might try to steal our thunder as it were. Or even scupper our operation. No, it is best they think of the Leviacra as eccentric British follies. In a decade's time, they will learn the truth soon enough. A new age of science will be upon us."

Such grand ideas and yet Cecil cringed at the thought of anyone wanting to amass that much energy. A volatile thing like psammeticum stored in tanks, sent through pipes like natural gas? The potential for devastation was incalculable. He'd already witnessed its unpredictability during the first time jump. But if that was their intent, at least it wasn't as sinister as most of the theories he'd heard over the years. At its heart, it was a scientific endeavour—a frightening and megalomaniacal one, but scientific nonetheless. And until he could figure out a way to escape his prison, he would aid them to that end, if only to help make the collection process safer for the men and women working on the project. Scientists all.

"And the towers we found in prehistoric Europe?" He began to fill in the gaps. "A large-scale attempt to harvest some invaluable comet-stuff brouhaha across time?"

"From what we have ascertained through geological study, several pieces of the largest Atlas comet broke off and hit the earth in the early Cretaceous Period. The comets themselves skimmed our atmosphere. The sublimation that occurred filled an entire hemisphere for months. When we first found the collapsed towers, I was as puzzled as you, Professor Reardon. But now it makes perfect sense. We are destined to achieve large-scale time travel, and our future successors in this endeavour will be even more ambitious than we have dreamed."

"Maybe, but they failed, didn't they? The towers were empty and decrepit. The dream you speak of seems fraught with more dangers than anyone can predict. Is there such a thing as too much ambition?"

She grinned cruelly. "You mean like trying to conquer fate in order to bring back one's deceased wife and son?"

Cecil's blood flamed. He jabbed a forefinger at her. "If you ever mention them again, I'll finish what I started in the factory." He thrust out his chin and began to rub it tauntingly. "You'd best stay out of my way from now on, Gorgon. I'm warning you."

"Enough!" Wallingford stepped between them, raised his hands in the manner of a traffic policeman. "I shall make all the arrangements you asked for, Professor. In the meantime, are you satisfied with our disclosure?"

"For now."

"Very well. We shall leave you to rest. Good day." He escorted his chunnering colleague out of the room, quietly berating her.

Cecil knew he'd won a victory. Why not gloat a little? "By the way," he called after them, "I'd like a full English breakfast, eggs over-easy, plenty of toast. Throw in a couple of hash browns, as well. See to it, will you?"

He laughed at Miss Polperro's snarl, then lay back against his pillow and surveyed his empty room. He thought of young Billy and Tangeni heading northward to Tromso, and Verity and Embrey wandering the deadly wilds of the Cretaceous, marooned forever unless he could somehow use his newfound influence and figure out how to reach them.

Until then, he could never truly rest, for he would be as much a prisoner as they.

One week later…

An arrowhead formation of geese flying in from the coast reminded Cecil of the first time he'd seen the Hatzegopteryx, high amid the clouds. They'd appeared no bigger than ordinary seabirds.

All life is about perspective, he thought. Dozens of airships littered the sky, and London city below seemed quiet, restful, oblivious.

He pulled the main gear lever on the side of his clockwork knee joint to its zero tension setting,

219

rendering it limp. Reclining on a deck chair on the eighty-first floor balcony outside his quarters, Cecil gave a contented sigh. It was the first sunny day since his incarceration in the tower and he was determined to make the most of it. He put on his spectrometer goggles and set the lenses to medium tint. A cool glass of sarsaparilla perspired on the stool next to him. First he opened yesterday's morning edition of the *Daily First,* one of the few newspapers that reported overseas news as thoroughly as events at home. He longed for news of Billy and his African aeronaut friends.

Killer Dinosaur To Be Displayed In London Museum

That front page headline struck him as the closing of a significant chapter in his life. The wild and indomitable baryonyx, master of its own world, was here a showpiece in a museum. Nothing now remained of his terrible adventure except in his mind. He skimmed through the article until he came to:

> "...*it cut a swathe of destruction across Southern England for three days and nights. The rampaging beast reached as far as Winchester before it was finally shelled by artillery during its slaughter of dozens of men and women engaged in a traditional countryside hunt.*
>
> "'*The baryonyx was the apex predator of its time,*' *said Miss Agnes Polperro, representative of the Leviacrum Council and one of the few survivors of the Westminster catastrophe. 'Its brief acquaintance with mankind is smeared with tragedy...for man and beast. It is fitting that everyone be allowed to see this great hunter in its original, ferocious glory, for as we are masters of the*

twentieth century, so too did he rule over prehistory. He is one of our great predecessors.'"

And yet, Embrey and Verity still had his kind to contend with. Would that Cecil had a second factory all to himself, where he could reproduce his time machine and bring them back post haste. But that secret he must keep indefinitely. The Council was looking over his shoulder at every turn, and they must not gain control of time travel. The five-past-eight phenomenon had already revealed the damage this meta-science, still in its infancy, could wreak upon the natural order of time.

"Professor, these just arrived for you." His personal assistant handed him a telegram and a slender package about fifteen inches by eight in size.

"Thank you."

"Can I get you anything else, sir?"

"No thank you. That will be all."

His assistant nodded and left. Cecil immediately retrieved the telegram from its already-opened envelope—those security stuffed shirts never let anything pass unmolested. The note read,

> PROFESSOR R HOPE YOU ARE WELL THOUGHT YOU MIGHT LIKE TO RESUME OUR LUNCHTIME GAME YOU WERE ON TOP OF BIGGEST LADDER STOP ROLLED FIVE PUTS ME BELOW YOU ON SQUARE DIRECTLY ABOVE THE BROWN SNAKE STOP YOUR TURN PROFESSOR

He leapt up in his seat and ripped the packaging off what had to be a Snakes and Ladders board. "Billy!"

But who had helped the lad send a telegram? Tangeni? Sorensen? This *had* to be some sort of cryptic message. Yet there was nothing unusual about the squares they'd indicated on the board. He checked the back. The only inscription, made in handwritten silver ink, read, Property of Ebony Eyes Bookstore.

It's a puzzle. Nothing to do with the actual board itself? All right, then it must be a code of some kind.

He scrutinized each and every word, paying particular attention to those that might appear normal to anyone else but unusual to him. *Lunch, biggest ladder, below you, directly above the brown snake, ebony eyes.* There were two brown snakes on the board. "The" brown snake had to have some other meaning. A literal one? What might that signify to Billy, Tangeni and himself? Snake? Dinosaur? *Brown dinosaur?* The baryonyx on display in the British Museum!

Directly above that? He wasn't allowed outside the tower and they must already know that. Above the museum itself then? That seemed to fit. He was on the tallest ladder—the Leviacrum tower—and they wanted him to look below, to the top of the British museum. Where? The roof? An airship hovering over it?

Excitedly, he pressed the lever in his knee joint to its walking gear, and the *clickety-click* signalled it was ready. He limped to the edge of the balcony and gazed down, instantly finding the large white-grey building he sought. He twisted the tiny wheels on the sides of his goggles, cycling through the different lenses until he had binocular vision. He adjusted the focus knob minutely, soon gaining a clear view of the museum roof. But there was no airship hovering overhead, and no sign of anyone or anything out of the ordinary atop the structure.

Frustrated, he fetched the telegram and studied it again.

Lunchtime game? It was yet a little after ten in the morning, a couple of hours shy of twelve noon.

He paced about the balcony impatiently, observing the museum roof every few minutes. The two hours seemed to last for days, but during that time he resolved that the handwritten silver name, Ebony Eyes Bookstore, had to be significant. The telegram code had been too intricate, too clever to leave any extraneous information, and the silver lettering stood out on the dark green cardboard backing like moonbeams on a duck pond.

Ebony eyes—dark eyes—sunglasses? Tinted spectrometer goggles?

If they were to send some sort of Morse Code message using flashes of light, one way to disguise it from prying eyes would be to emit light from a different spectrum, one undetectable by human vision. Infrared perhaps? Ultraviolet? He would try every lens in the goggles' cycle.

Twelve o'clock arrived and his nerves were already shredded with anticipation. He gazed down at the museum roof, fully expecting to see someone crouched atop it.

No one. Nothing. Had he misinterpreted the message?

Directly above the brown snake. He lifted his gaze higher and higher until he spied a small dirigible floating there, its propellers motionless. Several figures manned the deck, two of whom stood facing him against the port bulwark. They were too far away for him to recognise but he swore one of them was dark-skinned. Tangeni?

He carefully cycled through his spectrometer lenses, cursing his luck whenever one failed to produce the result he pined for. He was ready to rush inside his quarters and retrieve an oil lamp, start waving that to at least let his friends know he'd understood the telegram when, through his penultimate lens, the ocular Cavendish, he caught a blinding flash.

"Oh my God, of course! They're speaking the language of my machine—psammeticum refraction!"

It was indeed Morse Code, emitted with clarity and precision. They repeated the entire message twice more.

Professor, all is well. Hope you like your new leg. Billy, Tangeni and friends are safe with me. Have made tremendous progress with your temporal differentiator. Working on plan to rescue you. Difficult though. Spies are everywhere. Will return here at same time once a week. Hold tight. Wave if you understand. Sorensen.

He didn't wave right away. He wanted to prolong this wonderful moment—an illicit communication for his eyes only, from friends willing to brave the wrath of the Council itself. True friends. When he finally did wave, the two figures standing against the bulwark responded in kind.

As he watched the ship leave, a rousing warmth in the pit of his stomach rose to his throat and his eyes and ears, drawing glad tears. His heart lifted and remained afloat for hours. He barely ate that day and all the next. And despite the enormous responsibilities and the world-altering disclosures heaped upon him by the

Council, the only thing he truly cared about that week was obtaining two coloured counters and a single die.

He and Billy had a game to play. Snakes and Ladders. As when he'd waited indefinitely atop the rickety walkway above his great machine, Cecil was back to rolling his figurative die, hoping for an intervention. This time, it was not only Lisa and Edmond he must save but Verity and Embrey too.

He opened the board and set the pieces onto square one. The ups and downs were all ahead of him once more, but at least during this wait, he was not alone.

A small house spider scurried across the board, raising a smirk on Cecil's lips. *So miracles do happen.*

He considered how the game might end, if indeed it *could* ever end once it had begun. "Well, here goes." He slid the red counter forward.

He checked the telegram. The lad had just rolled a five...

Chapter 21

Embrey's Farewell

To whomever braves time to find this,

Come and seek us out! At the attached coordinates, you will discover the ruins of the only land-based Leviacrum tower left standing on this continent. We explore constantly, but that edifice is the closest we have to a home in prehistory. Yet it is not sufficient to keep us safe. The deadly creatures that reign over the outside world have made it imperative for us to delve underground, into the stupendous network of manmade tunnels fanning out from those coordinates. There is evidence of a technologically advanced civilization we believe may still exist deep within the bowels of this prehistoric realm. Might it hold the key to our salvation, to our return through time? Though we have unearthed a few of its secrets, we know not how or why it came to exist so far back in time. Even as I write this letter, the great towers rust and crumble. They will one day pass out of all human knowledge unless time is breached again and the breacher returns home. I therefore bequeath this mystery to you, dear traveller, in the event of our death. For we are captives here, driven beneath this vast, unconquered wilderness red in tooth and claw.

I am Lord Garrett Embrey, exile from the year 1908. Two years have passed since Professor Cecil Reardon, inventor of time travel, disappeared through time with two dozen others. We know nothing of their fates. Of the original survivors of our freak time jump, only I and one other remain. She is Verity Champlain, Captain of the Gannet airship, Empress Matilda, *and I love her with all my heart. That she returns those feelings is the solace that sustains me.*

I am securing this letter to the base of Big Ben in hope rather than expectation. We shall not return. Verity and I left these ruins because the area is too dangerous, but I suspect an errant time traveller would not happen upon this specific age by chance, and would therefore already know of the disappearance of Westminster. Let this be the start of your quest, then, dear traveller, and may we meet soon.

Be wary of the sound of thunder: the giant baryonyx roam these coasts; of sudden shadows: look up to the Hatzegopteryx, cruel kings of the skies; and venture across the lakes at your peril. As the decrepit Leviacrum towers illustrate, dinosaurs and man can never co-exist. Perhaps our erstwhile enemy, Agnes Polperro, was right and Nature only suffers interlopers—in time, in fate, in the food chain—temporarily before expelling them in its own subtle ways. Sooner or later, if Nature is governed by balance, the ebb and flow of time may swallow all man's attempts to change its course.

Our airship's next flight will be its last, as we have almost exhausted the hydrogen reserves. Verity and I will soon begin our next great adventure. For today, as the sun reached its zenith, we joined hands at the foot of Big Ben, a hallowed place where twentieth century grass still grows and time no longer chimes. While the sun's corona haloed the clock, we turned our faces toward heaven and plighted our troth beneath the eyes of God.

We live during the infancy of flowers, and she is my rose, the first and only one I shall ever love. We are without flag, without country, without sure means of survival. But we have each other, and that is more than enough.

What lies in store for us, I wonder.

Hopefully,
Garrett R. J. Embrey
Verity M. Embrey

Epilogue

Five Past Eight

1916

The howl of the wind outside his single porthole window kept Cecil awake, but barely. The days had grown long, interminable over the past several months without word from outside. Even the meagre telegrams that had arrived with clockwork regularity for many years, each containing but one number—the result of Billy's die roll for their epic games of Snakes and Ladders—had ceased. At least in his old quarters he'd been able to gaze out across London from his balcony, to pretend he was still a part of the world below. Here, on the 112th floor, he was nothing but a rusty old cog in the monotonous grind of a soulless machine.

His bushy beard was silver-white and reached down to his chest. His sore fingers, the prints worn away by too many cuts and abrasions during his obsessive fiddling with sharp edges and brittle lenses, hurt all day until he rested them in bed under his pillow. He slept more and more these days. No one seemed to complain, though, as his sharpness in the lab had long begun to wane. Truth be told, the scraps he'd fed the Council during his first few years spent in the tower, and his utter failure to reproduce his great machine—a deliberate failure—had relegated him to a kind of twilight position within the establishment. They treated him with benign neglect, neither resisting nor rewarding his small breakthroughs in other fields, despite his continued propensity for hard work.

It was genius they wanted—time travel or nothing—and he had let them down.

He'd slept peacefully each and every night with that knowledge.

The shadowy walls of his quarters slithered to life as he conjured, bittersweetly, his great adventure in prehistory. Airships swooped amid flying reptiles, diving bells plumbed the depths of a sea teeming with monstrous creatures, his friends fought with him and for him against impossible odds, and he grew to love them over time.

Ah, would that I were a young man again. I'd never go near a blasted laboratory. The world outside is much too interesting as it is. Am I right, Lisa? Am I right, Edmond?

Do everything within your power. Nothing else matters. You will never be complete if you don't try. Let God stop it if He must.

Hurtful words from long ago. He hadn't uttered them for years, but their sentiment haunted him like the scent of African lily perfume whenever he came across it in the tower's dining hall or the movie theatre. The wound was still tender. It had never healed.

He closed his eyes, changed sides on the bed and snuggled against a double pillow. Not even rain pelting the window could keep him awake now that he'd found something worth dreaming about. He imagined his wife and son running toward him on the lonely, rickety walkway overlooking his giant machine, moments before its cataclysmic reaction. But their smiles quickly dropped, and they yelled something at him in unison. No sound escaped their lips.

A terrific crash jolted him, and he sprang upright on the bed. He spun toward the open window, shielding his face from the violent gust of wind he was expecting. But none came. Nor was there any rain. The storm had ceased apoplectically. He checked the wall clock.

Ah, five past eight. Right on cue. But what broke the glass?

He got out of bed, put his single slipper on and walked over the shards to the window. Before he reached it, the slick, broad form of a man swung in through the gap, narrowly missing him. The intruder thudded sideways onto the carpet and gave an audible wince.

"What the devil? What do you mean by breaking in—"

"Quick, help me untie the rope," the interloper said as he leapt to his feet. A good six feet tall, he was young and handsome, with wide, straight shoulders and a rough and ready face, like a rugby player. He wore a navy blue slicker.

"Who are you? Tell me why I shouldn't throw you back out right now and pin a bill for the window to your backside."

"Five past eight. We've got seconds!" The man yanked at the knot around his waist, unfastening the rope, then he tossed it onto the floor. Next, he tore his slicker off to reveal a bizarre metallic contraption, about the size of a large rucksack, strapped to his back. He tightened the thick harness about the shoulders and around the waist of his khaki suit.

"What the hell is that? *Who are you?*"

231

The young man was too busy to answer. He clicked two levers on either side of the metal box and without warning snatched Cecil toward him by the wrists. "Here—when we jump, you'll need to wrap your arms *and* legs around me. Make sure the mechanical one is set to its walking gear so you can hold it bent around me. Is that clear?"

An escape! After all these years? "I understand." He didn't, but he would rather take this chance, perhaps his last, than spend the rest of his life cooped up in oblivion. "It's already set to that gear."

"Good. All right, here we go. Hold on tight, Cecil."

Cecil? Who called him that? None in the tower, and he hadn't spoken to a friend from the outside for going on a decade.

Ugh! His stomach vaulted into his brain as they jumped into a million suspended dew drops. The five past eight time glitch had rendered the storm a three dimensional, interactive tableau—spectacular and terrifying in equal measure. He crushed his limbs around the man. About a third of the way down, a whirring, clicking noise began in the metallic contraption. A dozen bulky silver rods shot out from either side. They immediately doubled in length, then tripled, becoming slenderer with each action. Finally, dovetailing metal lengths fanned out from each spine, forming streamlined wings. This new air resistance snatched Cecil and his rescuer from their deadly plummet and set them on a gliding path away from the tower.

The storm resumed with a shimmering stutter. A flash of lightning jived a million raindrops back to life, and they pounded the metal wings. Cecil clung even tighter as the birdman let go of him to pivot and angle the wings by means of levers at the base of the shell. He expertly guided them toward the deck of a medium-sized airship hovering a hundred feet over the Thames. A dozen African aeronauts waited with a giant net, to catch the fliers if they should overshoot their landing. Luckily, the birdman brought them down safely, skidding onto several wet mattresses arranged together on the quarterdeck.

"Well, how the hell do you do, Professor?"

Were he not already punchdrunk from too many shocks in too short a time, Cecil would have cried out with joy at the sight of his old Namibian friend, Tangeni, bounding over the mattresses wearing a slicker several sizes too big.

"Tangeni! I knew it was you behind this."

The African pilot, now sporting a short, black-grey beard, threw his arms around Cecil and wouldn't let go, and Cecil fancied he outdid that grip of affection with one of his own—one of the most heartfelt embraces he'd ever given.

"I thought you'd forgotten me, my friend."

"Never. We thought of everything to free you, but they were one step ahead of us at every turn. In the end, we took inspiration from our old friends, the flying dinosaurs. It was his crazy idea." He motioned to the birdman, who gave a bow. "The timing was everything—in and out before your captors knew a thing. And now that we have you back, there will be no stopping us. But come, they'll hunt us to the ends of the earth when they find out you've escaped."

Heavy rain thrashed the deck. Tangeni returned to the wheel, promising to share a brandy or five with Cecil as soon as he'd seen to their escape from London.

Meanwhile, the birdman fetched blankets, raincoats and sou'westers for Cecil and himself.

"I can never thank you enough, young man. And now will you *please* tell me your name."

His rescuer grinned, then gave a cheeky shrug. "'T weren't nothin'." The lad mimicked a Lancashire accent. The professor stood up straight, looked the young man over from head to toe, questing for further proof to support his unlikely assumption. But it couldn't be. This stranger no more resembled the boy he'd left behind in the factory wreckage than—

"I believe I'm a few squares ahead of you this time around, Cecil."

"Billy?"

"None other."

"My God, you've grown…unrecognisably."

"So have you."

They inched toward each other, shook hands. A more restrained and tentative reacquaintance than he'd shared with Tangeni, but harder to grasp. More filled with questions. With wonder. The boy had become the man Cecil had always dreamed of meeting. But it was not Edmond. It was Billy, the surrogate son of time travellers.

"Join me for a brandy?" Cecil asked.

The lad saluted, then placed his arm over the old professor's shoulders, leading him to Tangeni's cabin. "Aye, though I have to admit, I still prefer sarsaparilla. Don't tell anyone, though."

Inside the cabin smelled of incense and candle wax, while two amber oil lamps hung from the low, panelled roof. Three wooden chairs with cushioned seats faced each other in the centre, around which four tables had been arranged in a semi-circle. The latter were full of boxes and folders and curious archaeological specimens.

Tangeni noticed him studying the paraphernalia. "The expedition is all but underway, my good professor. You are the last to join—if you have no objection, of course."

He pursed his lips in mock contemplation. "Hmm, I will have to cancel my appointment with the barber first."

His two friends laughed. Billy poured them each a brandy.

"If it be to rescue Verity and Embrey, or even to find a small piece of that puzzle, I will gladly outdistance a thousand Phileas Foggs until we achieve it. To where do we fly?" Cecil asked.

"First to Marseilles." Billy plucked a fancy pipe from a drawer in one of the tables, packed it with rich-smelling tobacco from a leather pouch as he spoke. What an extraordinary transformation the lad had undergone. He was now an eloquent and self-sufficient young gentleman, not to mention ingenious for having orchestrated such a daring rescue. "Our sponsor awaits us there. We have over two dozen men and women ready to venture where few have ever set foot, including most of our aeronaut friends who survived the time jump."

"Smashing. And where lies this untamed land, may I ask?"

"In a remote region of Central Africa," Tangeni said. "That is where our next adventure begins, and a perilous one at that, if even half the legends are to be believed. It is a trail that leads into the bowels of the earth." He handed Cecil a flat, granite rock about the size of a fist.

Inscribed upon it was the Embrey family coat-of arms! "The clues all point to *Eembu* and Embrey, to something extraordinary having occurred in a world far beneath our feet."

"McEwan's antediluvian realm?" Breathlessly, Cecil swigged the remainder of his brandy and asked for a refill. "And time travel? Has Professor Sorensen—"

The African lifted his eyebrows. "He will have to explain that to you, I'm afraid. He has yet to emulate your great feat, but he says he is close to a breakthrough—one that could be the key to rescuing our friends marooned across time. He requires your collaboration."

"And he shall have it."

Tangeni raised his glass. "Cheers, Professor. Here's to your escape, and the return of old friends."

"Hear! Hear!" Cecil and Billy responded in chorus.

On the wall next to the starboard oil lamp hung a framed photograph. The date was marked 1907. It featured the entire crew of the *Empress Matilda,* arm in arm, forming three ranks. On the back row he recognized Kibo, the proud engine man wearing his smart waistcoat; Djimon, who had lost his life in the diving bell; and the two tall Kenyan women, Reba and Philomena. The middle row was full of faces he recognized, some of whom he might yet see again. And in the front row, centre, the unmistakable duo, whose great friendship and resourcefulness had triumphed over the direst moments of their prehistoric adventure, crouched side by side, grinning joyously. Verity's cropped red hair and beautiful face were indelible, her spirit insuperable. And Tangeni had proven his loyalty to her across two epochs.

236

On the left of the photograph hung a small portrait of Lord Garrett Embrey, the most impressive man Cecil had ever had the privilege of calling friend. Despite his youth, Embrey was already worthy of his father's title and others higher still, for he represented all that was best about the English under pressure. Despite all that had transpired to kill his compassion, he had never lost sight of the meaning of family.

He was a man after Cecil's heart. And they would meet again soon.

Let God stop it if He must.

About the Author

Robert Appleton is an English science fiction author with a penchant for interplanetary adventures and steampunk. His publishers include Harlequin Carina Press, and he also ghostwrites in various genres. In his free time he hikes, kayaks, and reads as many vintage sci-fi and adventure novels as he can get his hands on. His favorite books and films, like his own fiction, usually take place in the distant past or the far future. The night sky is his inspiration.

His work has been nominated for several awards, and in 2011 he won the EPIC Award for Best Historical Fiction.

Website: http://robertappletonbooks.com
Twitter: https://twitter.com/robertappleton

Printed in Great Britain
by Amazon